"Be careful. Don't marry someone just to give your daughter a father,"

Mick warned.

Laura looked surprised. "I don't intend to marry at all."

Mick's eyes seemed to turn fiercer than before, but he only gave her a quick nod. He gently touched her baby's cheek, then he took Laura's hand in his and studied it, as if remembering the hours they'd spent with their fingers linked.

Carefully he curled Laura's fingers closed. "Sleep," he whispered. "Rest. Have a good life."

Laura watched him disappear. Mick wasn't the first man who'd walked out of her life. Her father had walked away many times. Her baby's father had left. So she shouldn't feel sad to see Mick leave. Heavens, she didn't even know him! Even so, he wasn't a man she would easily forget.

"I hope there's nothing to this imprinting thing, sweetie," Laura crooned to her child. "Don't go getting attached to Mick. Just don't."

* * *

Maitland Maternity: The Prodigal Children
The Inheritance by Marie Ferrarella
Silhouette Single Title, August 2001
A Very Special Delivery by Myrna Mackenzie
SR #1540, September 2001
The Missing Maitland by Stella Bagwell
SR #1546, October 2001

Dear Reader,

September is here again, bringing the end of summer—but not the end of relaxing hours spent with a good book. This month Silhouette brings you six new Romance novels that will fill your leisure hours with pleasure. And don't forget to see how Silhouette Books makes you a star!

First, Myrna Mackenzie continues the popular MAITLAND MATERNITY series with *A Very Special Delivery,* when Laura Maitland is swept off her feet on the way to the delivery room! Then we're off to DESTINY, TEXAS, where, in *This Kiss,* a former plain Jane returns home to teach the class heartthrob a thing or two about chemistry. Don't miss this second installment of Teresa Southwick's exciting series. Next, in *Cinderella After Midnight,* the first of Lilian Darcy's charming trilogy THE CINDERELLA CONSPIRACY, we go to a ball with "Lady Catrina"—who hasn't bargained on a handsome millionaire seeing through her disguise....

Whitney Bloom's dreams come true in DeAnna Talcott's *Marrying for a Mom,* when she marries the man she loves— even if only to keep custody of his daughter. In *Wed by a Will,* the conclusion of THE WEDDING LEGACY, reader favorite Cara Colter brings together a new family—and reunites us with other members. Then, a prim and proper businesswoman finds she wants a lot more from the carpenter who's remodeling her house than watertight windows in Gail Martin's delightful *Her Secret Longing.*

Be sure to return next month for Stella Bagwell's conclusion to MAITLAND MATERNITY and the start of a brand-new continuity—HAVING THE BOSS'S BABY! Beloved author Judy Christenberry launches this wonderful series with *When the Lights Went Out...* Don't miss any of next month's wonderful tales.

Happy reading!

Mary-Theresa Hussey

Mary-Theresa Hussey
Senior Editor

Please address questions and book requests to:
Silhouette Reader Service
U.S.: 3010 Walden Ave., P.O. Box 1325, Buffalo, NY 14269
Canadian: P.O. Box 609, Fort Erie, Ont. L2A 5X3

A Very Special Delivery

MYRNA MACKENZIE

SILHOUETTE *Romance*®

Published by Silhouette Books

America's Publisher of Contemporary Romance

Special thanks and acknowledgment are given
to Myrna Mackenzie for her contribution to the
MAITLAND MATERNITY: PRODIGAL CHILDREN series.

 SILHOUETTE BOOKS

ISBN 0-373-19540-0

A VERY SPECIAL DELIVERY

Books by Myrna Mackenzie

Silhouette Romance

The Baby Wish #1046
The Daddy List #1090
*Babies and a Blue-Eyed
    Man* #1182
The Secret Groom #1225
*The Scandalous Return of
    Jake Walker* #1256
Prince Charming's Return #1361
Simon Says... Marry Me! #1429
At the Billionaire's Bidding #1442
Contractually His #1454
The Billionaire Is Back #1520
Blind-Date Bride #1526
A Very Special Delivery #1540

*The Wedding Auction

Silhouette Books

Montana Mavericks
Just Pretending

MYRNA MACKENZIE,

winner of the Holt Medallion honoring outstanding literary talent, has always been fascinated by the belief that within every man is a hero, and inside every woman lives a heroine. She loves to write about ordinary people making extraordinary dreams come true. A former teacher, Myrna lives in the suburbs of Chicago with her husband—who was her high school sweetheart—and her two sons. She believes in love, laughter, music, vacations to the mountains, watching the stars, anything unattached to the words *physical fitness* and letting dust balls gather where they may. Readers can write to Myrna at P.O. Box 225, LaGrange, IL 60525-0225.

THE MAITLANDS:

MEGAN MAITLAND:
Matriarch of the Maitland family. Her life had been filled with sorrow, excitement and joy. Once she was reunited with her long-lost son, she'd thought all would be well. But now strange things were happening at her clinic, and she wasn't sure who was behind the mystery. Was her dream of a maternity clinic going to fail?

JANELLE MAITLAND:
The oldest of black sheep Robert Maitland's children. Ambitious and grasping, she'd stolen and blackmailed and lied to gain the Maitland money. She'd been captured and sent to jail, but she has broken out. Could she be behind the incidents? And was she representative of all the prodigal Maitlands?

RAFE MAITLAND:
The youngest of Robert's children. Hardworking rancher. He'd always lived life alone, but in the past few months he'd acquired a daughter—and a wife! Now he would do anything to protect his family....

LAURA MAITLAND:
Robert's third child. Vulnerable new mother. She'd swallowed her pride to ask for help with her child. She'd vowed never to depend on another man again, but Mick Hannon was very hard to resist....

LUKE MAITLAND:
Robert's second child. Even investigative reporter Blossom Woodward couldn't find anything out about his past. Or his future...

Chapter One

"I—I'm sorry, but I think I've waited too long. Please help me. I'm going to have my baby. Right now."

The soft, shaky words caught Mick Hannon's attention and he spun from where he'd been reviewing a set of blueprints outside Austin's Maitland Maternity clinic to see a pale, delicate woman with long brown hair swaying on her feet. Her eyes were wide with distress, her arms cradled her abdomen. She was staring beseechingly at one of the gardeners who'd been trimming the bushes at this end of the long drive.

Just at that moment, the woman sucked in a deep breath and a low moan spilled from her pale lips. Her knees began to buckle.

The unfortunate gardener's eyes went round and scared. He didn't move.

"Hell," Mick said, and he threw off his hard hat and rushed forward, slipping his hand behind the woman's back to support her as she began to slide downward.

"Easy, darlin'," he crooned kneeling as he helped her to sit down. "Easy, now. We'll get you inside where the doctors will take care of you." With his arm looped around her, the silk of her hair drifted against his neck, soft and smelling of flowers. In spite of her condition, she felt as light as froth. But as she leaned her weight against his shoulder, she stiffened, and he felt the tension of her body against his side. The contraction rippled through her, tightening her slender arms and legs. He looked straight into huge green eyes glazed with pain. A light sheen of perspiration had dampened a few strands of her hair, making them catch against her lips.

A sense of panic and urgency filled him. This might be a maternity clinic, but he was only here to add a wing to the building. Pregnant women and babies were outside the realm of what he knew or wanted to know.

"I'm—all right," she said as if she'd read his very thoughts, and he wondered if he'd spoken without realizing it. "Don't worry. This is—the way all women do it, I think. It's supposed to hurt." But her teeth sank into her lip and all he could think was that it wasn't fair that a woman this tiny should have to bear a pain this big for a baby that would come back in sixteen years and break her heart fifty thousand times.

He slid in closer, meaning to lift her, hoping it was the right thing to do and that he wouldn't hurt her.

But she shook her head slightly, gasping. "I think— I think maybe I should get up and walk. All the books tell you to walk,'' she said in a strained voice the size of a field mouse.

Mick duly noted her need to be in control of her situation. He also noted how pale her skin was against her dark lashes. Gently, he adjusted his grip on her, trying to make her more comfortable, as she struggled to rise.

"Shh. Be still. You can walk later,'' he suggested. "After the doctors say it's all right.''

And right then, her body quivered and tightened and he could tell the roll of pain was gathering speed and depth. Her teeth clicked together as she held on to the scream he was sure she needed to give vent to.

"Hold on,'' he said gruffly, trying not to jostle her and hurt her any more than she already was. "I'll get a doctor. Don't move.'' Carefully he helped her to settle back against one of the pillars of the clinic's entrance, then dashed off to find help.

The doors of the clinic slid back with an electric swish, and Mick strode into the waiting room, taking in his surroundings. There was no doctor, only a young receptionist in serious conversation with Megan Maitland, CEO of Maitland Maternity and matriarch of the Maitland clan, one of the first people he'd learned to recognize when he arrived in Austin a week ago. The tension in his shoulders relaxed ever so slightly. Megan probably knew a lot about women on the verge of giving birth.

"Ms. Maitland, please. There's a woman outside who needs you,'' he said, and to his relief, Megan only looked startled for a second before she nodded and rushed out the door in front of him.

Mick followed close behind her, but his heart nearly stopped beating when he saw his pregnant beauty standing on unsteady legs and trying to move toward the building. Her face was pale, her eyes stricken. She slipped, and Megan rushed forward, catching her as they both nearly went down. The older woman gave the younger one her strength.

The pregnant woman shuddered and spoke, her words coming out in a garbled whisper. She closed her eyes and once again struggled to rise.

This wouldn't do. To hell with what the doctor's would advise—or anything else. Mick stepped in and scooped this fragile, valiant woman into his arms, holding her close.

He glanced down at her. "You all right?"

She opened her eyes and nodded tightly, then took a gasping breath of air as she looked toward Megan.

"Now, blow it out," he directed, when it seemed as if the air had gotten trapped in her lungs.

She did, then took another breath and let it out, then another. She stole another quick glance toward the woman who was a legend in the baby birthing business.

"Okay. I'm—I'm…better now," the soft bundle of woman he was holding managed to say, and his attention was drawn to those green eyes that were now gazing straight into his own. "I—thank you for being here, and for helping me, but—I think I've finally pulled myself together now." Her glance took in both Mick and Megan. "I'm sorry that I acted so—so—"

"Pregnant?" he guessed with a hint of a smile.

She tried to smile back, but it was obvious that she

was very weak. How in the world had she even managed to get here? ''Pregnant,'' she agreed. ''And stupid in not realizing my back pains were real contractions. But—I'm sure I'm fine now. You can put me down. Now that I've caught my breath I can walk,'' she said. She pushed against his chest with those delicate, fluttery hands of hers. A fruit fly would have made more of an impact. Her breath still sounded a bit labored, and he made no move to follow her instructions.

He also noticed that she wasn't wearing a ring. So? Maybe she didn't have a husband…or maybe, well, there were plenty of pitiful excuses for husbands around. His father and stepfather had been cut from that very cloth, but with that thought, his beauty's baby chose that moment to move into action again. Mick felt the quick catch in her breath. Tension climbed his body as he clutched the woman close.

''Let's get her inside,'' Megan said. A chill trickle of fear ran sprints up and down his spine. ''We'll get her into a wheelchair and into the delivery room.''

But the lady in his arms clutched tighter as the pain climbed and Megan shook her head.

''All right, never mind the wheelchair—or protocol. Come with me. I've had three babies of my own and I'm definitely of the opinion that when a woman is in labor, she deserves to be given whatever she needs. Right now, Mr. Hannon, this woman appears to need you.''

For half a second, Mick wondered how the woman knew his name. But then, he'd heard she made a point of learning the names of those who worked for her.

With the recent acts of vandalism at the clinic, she'd want to be able to identify the temporary employees. That wasn't good. The less the Maitlands knew of him the better. He should really leave now that he'd gotten his silken-haired beauty some help.

He opened his mouth to suggest that he needed to get back to work, but then the woman in his arms closed her eyes. Her delicate jaw tensed. And the gates of reason swung shut with a muffled click. He reluctantly nodded his agreement to Megan. He would stay here a few minutes longer.

Briskly Megan led the way into the clinic, past the cool pastel reception area and down a corridor into a birthing room decorated in pale blue and white with honey-toned wood accents. It looked more homey than the hotel room Mick was staying in right now.

Gently, he deposited the lady in his arms in a cushioned rocker, but she was apparently beyond noticing her surroundings. Indeed, she had curved those slender hands around his fingers and was holding on for dear life as if only he could save her. She looked up at him with deep distress in her eyes and, automatically, he dropped to his knees, his jeans sinking into the plush carpet. He kept his eyes on hers and let her try to crush his big hands with her small ones.

"It's all right," he said. "Hold on to me."

"You're going to do just fine," Megan said. "Mick and I are going to make sure of that."

For half a second Mick's concentration broke. Belatedly, he remembered what he'd known for years. He was no woman's champion, and he had excellent reasons to steer clear of tempting women who were nesting. Still, right now his reservations, his hard-and-fast rules for living his life would have to be set aside. He turned his attention back to his damsel in distress.

"You'll be fine, sunshine," he whispered reassuringly. "And so will baby sunshine."

His lady gave a quick, chopping nod of her head, then simply stared back at him fiercely as if he possessed some secret he knew he didn't have. She held herself almost motionless, only her never-let-go grip on his fingers revealing the battle being fought within her body.

She's too still, Mick thought. As if she weren't even alive. "Ms. Maitland?" he asked.

"Breathe," Megan directed the woman. "Like this." And soon Mick was breathing along with her, his pregnant beauty watching his every move and taking her cues from him.

When the contraction finally passed, she looked down at her hands, at her onion-white knuckles and her choking grip on his fingers. Carefully she opened her hands and released him.

"Sorry," she whispered weakly. "Thank you." Her voice was small, some might say prim.

"Don't mention it." He softened his usually low, gruff voice as much as he could. "You're much too small to hurt me."

"I'm sure this isn't how you planned to spend your afternoon," she said, licking dry lips.

He handed her the glass of water Megan passed to him. "Hey, sweet stuff, you're making my day a lot more interesting than it might have been. It's not all that often that a man gets to take a beautiful woman in his arms on his coffee break. I'll be the envy of my men.'' From somewhere he managed to dredge up a reassuring smile.

"Thank you for being kind." An entrancing trace of pink tinged the lady's cheeks. She looked away. As if she thought he would repeat tales of her most private moments to his men.

Which reminded him, his co-workers would be thinking he'd gone back to Dallas and left them behind.

"Excuse me, Ms. Maitland, but..." He nodded toward the window, not wanting to mention his concern and worry his lovely little mother-to-be even more.

Megan nodded. "I already had our receptionist let your crew know we had commandeered your services. You don't mind?"

He minded, but he could tell that the beauty was listening. The truth was that he'd spent his whole adult life avoiding women who represented hearth and home. In fact, the last time he'd been this intimate with a woman, he'd been intent on making sure he didn't *make* any babies while he took his pleasure. He'd certainly never thought to see the inside of a birthing room.

Shouldn't be here now, he thought, but he turned his attention to the woman and Megan, who was, essentially, his employer these days.

"You came in alone," Megan said to the woman. "Have you met with one of the doctors here before?"

A vehement shaking of the head followed. "I just arrived in town today."

"Do you...have someone meeting you here?"

Those soft green eyes looked suddenly unsure. "I'm here alone. I'm—not married, if that's what you mean. But I'm okay. Really, I can do this on my own," the woman added quickly, looking at Mick.

In spite of her uncomfortable condition, she managed to raise that delicate chin in an attempt at bravado. Her skin was dewy and pale, a startling contrast to pink lips, dark hair and the vulnerable but rich green of her eyes. The thought that some man had tasted those lips, brushed his fingers through that silken hair and gazed into those eyes as he joined his body to hers nine months ago skimmed through Mick's mind, and his breath snagged in his throat. Instantly he felt like even more of a heel than the jerk who'd left her to deal with the consequences.

But she was still staring at him, waiting. Obviously she wanted him to leave. No surprise. This was an intimate situation. He could understand her reluctance to share it with a stranger. She'd be even more reluctant to have him here, and so would Megan if they knew who he was and that he was at Maitland Maternity under false pretenses.

"You're quite a gutsy lady," he said with a nod of admiration at his dark-haired woman. "Make sure and say hello to your little one when she arrives."

He started to rise, but Megan shook her head.

"Not yet," she said, before turning to her patient.

"I admire your determination, dear, but I hope you'll reconsider," Megan said gently. "I've gone through labor alone, and believe me, it's much better to have someone coach you along, even if they're inexperienced. Mr. Hannon's been given the green light to stay. It's unorthodox to have him here, perhaps, but we'll find him a help. You will help, won't you?''

He wanted to say no, but there didn't seem to be any answer but yes. If he left, who would she hold on to when the pain came? Megan's fingers looked much too fragile. The nurse who had entered moments ago had other details to see to.

"I'll stay," he agreed.

"That wouldn't be fair," the woman was saying. "You just had the misfortune to be in the wrong place at the wrong time. And really—I don't need anyone. I *want* to do this by myself."

He really ought to be relieved at her dismissal. The thought of staying here and watching this woman suffer ranked right at the top of the list of things he didn't want to do today or ever. But the memory of that lost, frightened look in her eyes was still fresh.

"I'd consider it an honor if you'd let me stay," he said, countering her request. "Who knows when I might need to know how to do this again?" he tried to tease, and it seemed to work.

"See there, dear. You'd be doing Mick a favor for when he has his own children," Megan agreed brightly.

Even though he'd never have any children, Mick thought.

Still, when the next contraction started, he reached out for her hand and welcomed the soft pads of her fingertips pressing into his skin. He stroked his thumb over her palm.

"Don't worry, sweetheart," he whispered. "You're the bravest woman in the city right now. Your baby's going to be lucky to get someone who's such a fighter.''

He slipped his hand behind her and rubbed small circles over her slender lower back as Megan directed him to.

The woman looked up at him helplessly.

''Hold on to me,'' he whispered. ''Let me help you. Yell at me if it helps. Tell me what you think of the male race,'' he urged when she simply clamped her hands down harder on him.

That made those green eyes flash. ''Men—I—yes. I—I just can't say. I don't want to talk now. I can't think straight,'' she choked out, but the words were said with such intensity that Mick hoped that she'd found some release.

Finally the contraction slid away. The woman slumped back in her chair. She cast a slightly guilty look at Mick, but not too guilty, he noted. There was a little resentment thrown in, as well.

He grinned at her. ''I almost got you to swear, didn't I?'' he asked.

''I never swear.''

''But you wanted to. And you didn't think about the pain while I was irritating you, did you?''

A wan smile lifted one corner of her lips. ''Now I'm on to you,'' she said tiredly. She looked down. ''Thank you,'' she said in a small voice. ''You ever consider doing this for a living?''

''I'll take it up with my boss. If any of the guys go into labor, maybe he'll make use of my services.''

Megan chuckled. She'd been coaching Mick during the contraction, but now she took up the clipboard the nurse had carried in with her and turned to her patient. "Well, dear, we really seem to be doing things backward today," she said, "but we *do* need to get a bit of information from you, now that we have some breathing space."

The woman seemed to gather a cloak of pride around her. She withdrew her hand from Mick's. Her fingers absently pleated a fold of her yellow maternity top. "You want to know who I am."

"For starters, yes," Megan said gently.

The woman took a long, deep breath. For a minute Mick thought she was going to have another contraction, but then she squared her shoulders and nodded slowly.

"I'm Laura Maitland," she said in that soft voice.

To her credit, Megan barely blinked. "From Las Vegas?"

Laura's body stiffened slightly, as if someone had traced a probing finger down her spine. "Yes. A long time ago."

"My late husband William's niece," Megan said. "I've been trying to get in touch with you."

Laura looked away.

"Yes, I know. I'm—afraid my family hasn't been very good to yours. I can understand why you'd want to confront my brothers and me. Our family has wronged you terribly."

Mick had read the story about how Janelle Maitland had kidnapped Megan's grandson. He knew of the eventual recovery of the child. He'd heard that Janelle had a sister.

"If I could change the past, I would," Laura whispered to Megan. "I don't expect you to welcome me. I wouldn't have come at all if I'd had anywhere else to go, but there wasn't much money and no insurance. I was worried about my baby, and…well, I've seen news of the clinic on television and you had sent me that invitation to the Maitland Christmas reunion, so I just…headed here. I—I can't pay you right away, but my baby's birth won't be charity, I promise. If you let me have my child here, I'll make it up to you, somehow."

A long silence followed. Laura turned sad, worried eyes to the blue-eyed matriarch of the Maitland clan.

Megan laid a gentle hand on the woman's shoulder. "My dear, any woman in the world would ask for help when her child is at stake. I've been a woman in need myself, so please don't distress yourself. Of course you'll have your baby here. And please, don't worry about the other just now. It wasn't your doing, and the past doesn't matter one whit when there's a baby being born."

But Mick knew the past did matter. If a person forgot his history, he made mistakes. He could hurt people. It helped to remember that and to know which paths were open to a man and which were closed.

But then the nurse looked at him, and his only thought was to get out of the way so that she could help prepare Laura for what lay ahead.

He took Laura's hand into his own and touched his lips to the soft skin of her palm. "You're doing great, angel," he told her with a smile. "I'm just going to leave you to the pros now. Don't swear too much at the medical professionals," he teased.

But she hung on to his hand when he started to pull away.

"Thank you, Mr. Hannon," she said solemnly, and he knew she thought he meant to slip away permanently.

Indeed, when he exited the room, he thought she was right. He did his best to think of Laura Maitland only as an interesting incident in his day, not as a real, living, flesh-and-blood, steel-and-silk woman.

Probably no one would blame him for simply going back to his job. It was the smart thing to do. He had come to Austin for a good cause, but to accomplish his goal, he needed to remain anonymous, in the shadows. Something as unusual as a construction worker helping out in the delivery room just might attract speculation.

"Be smart, Hannon. Don't go letting sentiment or an overabundance of testosterone lead you around. A man in your position would do well to stay far away from Laura Maitland," he whispered to himself.

He said that. He meant it, but then he heard a low moan. Laura was having another contraction. She would be scared.

Mick shoved the door open and entered the room uninvited.

Chapter Two

When Mick Hannon strode back into the birthing room, all broad shoulders and determination, Laura's tension level dropped several notches. His intense, blue-eyed gaze bypassed the doctor, the nurse and Megan, targeting Laura, where she now lay on the bed. She stared back as the man's presence filled the room. He moved to her without asking anyone for permission or instruction, and the rest of the room fell away. The pain was no less. In fact, the great rolling waves biting into her were stronger than ever. Still, three seconds earlier she had doubted her ability to stay sane all the way to the end of the contraction. Now she knew that she would at least do that.

He held out his hands and she reached for the lifeline. She stared into his eyes and concentrated on that deep blue flecked with silver. She breathed when he told her to breathe.

When her mind wavered and she thought she would

go crazy with pain, she squeezed his hands harder and strove to blot out everything but the gravelly tones of his voice as he whispered encouragement.

"You're amazing," he told her, and that one statement distracted her. It was enough to keep her holding on for five seconds longer, even though she knew better than to believe the pretty lies that men offered.

Hours later, Laura took one last tired glance into Mick Hannon's fierce blue eyes, gripped his fingers tightly, and with a cry of pain and exhaustion, pushed her child into the world and into Dr. Abby Maitland's waiting hands.

For two seconds, there was total silence as the wonder of life renewing itself filled the room. Then a tiny, angry cry rang out.

"Thank heaven and Texas," Mick said on a breath. He shook his head in amazement as Laura fell back against the bed and gazed tiredly up at him.

"You did it, lady," he whispered, leaning over her, and he gently smoothed her damp hair back from her brow. "Congratulations. You brought your baby safely into the world."

His words were so intimately low that for a moment Laura thought he was going to pull her close in a hug, or maybe he was even going to kiss her. The look in his eyes was that intense. But then the baby let out another cry and Mick took a deep, audible breath. He stopped his forward momentum and straightened to his full and considerable height.

"You're okay, aren't you?" he asked quietly.

She tried to nod her head.

"You're tired," Megan said sympathetically.

"I'm okay," Laura managed to say. "My baby. Is my baby—"

"She's perfect," Megan said with a soft smile. "Your daughter is so perfect. So beautiful." Her tone was awed and reverent, as if this experience was new for her all over again. Laura noted for the first time that the woman had shed the jacket to a suit that could only have been designed by Donna Karan. Her lovely hair had grown a bit mussed. Megan had jumped right in to help, as if she were a midwife, not a CEO. Now she looked tired but pleased. Laura understood why expectant mothers flocked to her clinic.

"Isn't this just the most precious child you've ever seen, Mick?" Megan was saying, and Laura turned again to look at the man, the total stranger who had helped Megan coach her through the most painful, rewarding hours of her life. For the first time she saw him clearly, not through a haze of pain. His black hair was rumpled where he'd brushed long, lean fingers through it countless times. The blue chambray of his shirt clung to his broad shoulders damply in spite of the air-conditioned room. His mouth looked incredibly soft, even as his lips parted slightly in bewildered amazement.

Laura gazed at him, waiting for his answer.

For the first time he looked...awkward. "She's a feisty little thing," he finally said. "And she's definitely got all her fingers and toes. Cute little fingers and toes, too. Even some hair on her head."

Laura wished she had the energy to laugh. She knew just how red and wrinkled and, well, not particularly beautiful most babies would seem to the average male.

While she waited for the doctor and nurse to finish with her baby, she smiled her gratitude at Mick. He was trying so hard to think of something positive to say.

But then he looked at the baby again and his eyes darkened with concern. "Is she really supposed to be that tiny?" he asked Dr. Abby. "Surely not. She's not much bigger than my cupped hands. How could anything that small cause so much trouble?"

Megan chuckled. "I'm sure she'll cause her mother a great deal more trouble before she's grown up. It's one of the wonderful things children do, you know." Laura had the feeling she meant every word.

When Dr. Maitland gave Laura her baby to cuddle close to her, Laura captured one tiny flailing hand and kissed the softness of her child's skin. A sudden sense of wonder, of having been involved in a small miracle, of having been given a gift too overwhelmingly generous for anyone to ever deserve, filled her. Unbelievable as it seemed, this baby had come from her, from inside her own body. This vulnerable, amazing child was hers to keep and care for and love. From a relationship that had ended ugly, from an experience that had threatened to overpower her, had come this amazing, sweet little being. Gratitude filled her soul.

She looked up into Mick's dark blue eyes. He was gazing at her and her daughter intensely, with a sense of awe and disbelief that rivaled her own, and with an unmistakable air of...reservation. As if he wanted to move closer and edge away at the same time.

Laura smiled at him. She held out her free hand.

"Thank you for helping me," she said weakly. "I was pretty scared there for a while, I think."

He shook his head. "You were pretty brave, I think, and no thanks are needed. You were the one who did all the work."

He took a deep breath and now she was absolutely sure that he wanted to step away, that now that the crisis had passed he wanted to get out of here fast. Well, he'd definitely earned his freedom. He probably had plenty of important tasks waiting for him, maybe even a woman wondering where he was. Of course he would have a woman, and of course there was no reason for him to have to stay any longer, but she couldn't let him go without letting him know just how important his presence had been.

She reached out and took one of his big callused hands, turning it over. In spite of her exhaustion or maybe because of it, a frisson of sensation spiraled down her arm and headed straight through her body when her skin met his. Strange that she should react to the man now when she'd been gripping these same hands for hours, thinking only that they represented safety and strength. Small red indentations marred his palms.

"You let me dig my fingernails into you, and you didn't complain," she said softly. "The guys on the crew are sure going to wonder what you've been doing." Exhausted as she was, she wanted to do this right. She knew that once he walked out that door, his part in her life would be past. But it had been such an important part. She wanted him to leave feeling good about this experience, not uncomfortable. He'd teased her earlier when she'd been embarrassed. How could she do any less?

"No problem. I'll just tell them I've been wrestling with a tigress," he promised. "A courageous, determined, green-eyed tigress. That'll make them wonder. In fact, I should be grateful to you, Ms. Maitland. You've probably made my reputation. I disappear for hours and come back scratched and barely able to think straight."

She couldn't help smiling. "Ah, we've done a good day's work then, love," she told her baby, kissing the top of her head.

"You have," Megan agreed, and Laura turned her attention to the beaming eyes of the woman still standing beside her.

Tears came to Laura's eyes. "Thank you for helping me," she said softly. "I see now why your clinic has such a good reputation, even among the rich and famous. Do you always give such personal service?"

Abby Maitland chuckled.

For the first time Megan Maitland looked mildly flustered. "Any woman would have done the same. And you are family. Now, you rest. I'll see you around, my dear," she said, tucking her hair back into place and smoothing her jacket as she repaired whatever damage had been done. "Come on, Abby," she told her daughter. "Let's let Laura have some time to get acquainted with her baby."

Mick started to move away, too, as the women filed out the door, but Laura reached out and touched his arm.

He stopped.

She realized that they were totally alone for the first time since this ordeal had begun. She realized what an incredibly, stunningly handsome man he was. The kind of man who undoubtedly had women hitting on him every day and not because they needed a labor coach, either.

"I know I'll see Megan again, but I doubt we'll meet again, Mr. Hannon. I'd like to repay you in some way. And please don't say it's not necessary," she said as he opened his mouth. "As nice as you've been, I know this couldn't have been on your list of things to do on a busy workday."

He gave her that "are you crazy?" look that some men are so very good at. "Top of the list," he insisted. "Holding a beautiful woman's hand is always a pleasure."

She smiled. "You're quite a charmer, Mr. Hannon, but seriously, let me do something for you. At least give me your address so I can send you an appropriate thank-you gift."

His lips thinned into a stubborn line. "I don't live in Austin. I'm just in town for the duration of the job."

"And there's nothing I can do for you?"

He looked down at where her baby was sleeping on her stomach.

"If she were a boy, I'd gladly name her Mick," she said gently.

He shook his head. "Thank you, but you wouldn't want to do that. Just…be careful. Don't marry the first man who comes along just to give her a father. The results can sometimes be disastrous."

She widened her eyes. "I suppose you don't have to worry, then. I don't intend to marry at all."

His eyes seemed to turn fiercer than before, but he only gave her a quick nod. "Then that won't be a problem, will it?"

He gently touched just the tip of his finger to her baby's cheek, then he took her hand in his and studied it, as if remembering the hours they'd spent with their fingers linked.

Carefully he curled her fingers closed. He lay her hand back on her child. "Sleep," he whispered. "Rest. Have a good life, Ms. Maitland."

And quietly he turned to leave her. She watched his broad back disappear.

He wasn't the first man she'd watched walk out of her life. Her father had walked away many times. Her baby's father had been offended that she would even ask for him to consider taking home the daughter of a Vegas showgirl to meet his family.

So it shouldn't have made her feel a bit sad to see Mick Hannon leaving. Heavens, she didn't even know him. She certainly didn't want him to stay. She didn't want any man in her life anymore, especially one as wickedly handsome and tempting as Mick Hannon.

Even so, he wasn't a man she would turn around and forget by morning. Lifting her hand, palm up, she examined the skin that looked no different than it had this morning. But something had changed. The sensation of Mick Hannon's strong fingers tangled with hers lingered.

"I hope there's nothing to this imprinting thing, sweetie," Laura crooned to her child. "Remember, you're not a baby duck, angel. The first man you see isn't going to be your father. So don't go getting attached to Mr. Hannon. Just don't.''

Laura woke to the sound of frantic whispers outside her room. She immediately looked toward the small bassinet beside her bed. Her baby had awakened several times during the night, but now she was sleeping quietly. Whatever was going on, it didn't have anything to do with her child.

The whispers rose a pitch, and she looked expectantly toward the door.

"You can't go in there, Mr. Maitland. Visiting hours won't be for several more hours.''

But the door swung back, anyway, and a tall, dark-haired, green-eyed man moved in.

Laura blinked several times, then a smile lifted her lips. "Rafe? It can't really be my baby brother, can it? You're here?'' She sat up in a rush before remembering what a battering her body had taken yesterday.

A tiny gasp escaped her, and Rafe rolled his eyes and strode to her bedside, catching her up in a gentle hug. "You get out of that bed and I'll show you that I'm still bigger than you even if you're two years older. And you bet I'm here. A hundred rattlesnakes couldn't keep me away once I heard the rumors about what had been going on here yesterday. I've been trying to reach you for weeks. Ever since I got that first invitation from Megan to come here for the family reunion.''

"Mine had to be forwarded several times," she admitted. After Greg, her fiancé, had made it clear he wasn't going to be a husband or father, she'd left California, needing a fresh start and a place to heal in private.

Rafe's eyes turned fierce. "You could have told me," he said, his voice breaking slightly as he looked toward the baby. "Hon, why didn't you tell me? We talked on the phone often enough up until you moved and we lost touch a few months ago."

Laura felt the threat of tears as she tried to find some answer that would make sense. She shook her head.

"Maybe because even though I hated Greg for a while after he left me, I didn't want him dead. And don't tell me that you wouldn't have wanted to exact a little retribution."

Rafe opened his mouth, then closed it, his eyes angry. He couldn't tell her that he wouldn't have tried to protect her.

Which led her to the deeper reason she hadn't turned to her brothers for help. After her shipwrecked romance, she'd really needed to prove that she could survive alone. She just couldn't be like her mother, leaning on the nearest man in order to stand up. And both her brothers were men made for leaning on.

"I would have told you soon," she said. "Just as soon as I got settled. I'm here, aren't I?" she asked, trying to smile.

He took her hand, studying it as if he didn't believe she was real. It had been weeks since they'd talked on the phone, months since they'd seen each other.

"You didn't have to go through childbirth alone."

"I didn't." She'd had Mick. She'd leaned on him. The truth was uncomfortable.

"I heard." There was hurt in his voice.

"I'm sorry, Rafe," she said, meaning every word. "It's just that you and Luke and I have been on our own for a long time. Sometimes we just need to go underground." Like wounded animals who protected themselves by hiding, even from those they loved.

"Yes, we do tend to do that, but two of us weren't pregnant," Rafe pointed out. "At least I'm not. Who knows about Luke? Nobody's heard from him lately."

In spite of Rafe's attempt at a joke, a sad, awkward silence followed. Concern for Luke hung in the air.

"Oh, Rafe, I've missed you," Laura said with a small, sobbing croak.

And he caught her close and kissed her hair. "I've missed you, too, hon," he said, his voice thick. "Tons. We've got a lot of catching up to do. I want you to meet my wife, Greer. She's Megan's assistant. That's how I heard you were here."

Laura pulled back, her eyes opening wide. "You're married? You? That's…that's wonderful. I can't wait to meet the woman who finally tamed you. I guess you know I have someone for you to meet, too." She picked up her baby, who was beginning to stir. "Meet your uncle Rafe, Meggie. He's a big guy, but he's pretty sweet most of the time."

Rafe grinned. "Don't tell anyone she said that part about being sweet, little one," he told his niece, hesitantly touching just the baby's blanket. "My friends might not understand. She's so tiny," he said with awe, and Laura couldn't forget a black-haired man with fierce blue eyes saying just the same thing. She hurriedly pushed the thought away.

"She'll grow, I think," Laura promised.

"Meggie?" he asked.

Laura smiled then and shrugged. "Megan Maitland didn't have to let me stay here, but she did. What's more, a nurse told me that the reason Megan is so sympathetic to single mothers is because her first baby's father deserted her. Just like me. She made her way alone just as I want to."

"She's a good woman."

"I know. Janelle shouldn't have tried to hurt her."

Rafe's eyes darkened. "Our sister did lots of damage. You need to know that. Things have been happening at the clinic. Sabotaged water pipes. A small fire. Janelle's on the loose, and suddenly both her sister and brother show up in Austin."

Laura sucked in a deep breath. "Do you think that Janelle is behind all these attempts to sabotage the clinic?"

He shrugged. "Janelle's capable of some pretty sleazy stuff. She convinced Megan that the baby she'd thought had died at birth was Janelle's husband, when Janelle knew all along that Clarise O'Hara and her husband had illegally adopted Connor right after he was born. She knew exactly where the real Connor was and didn't tell Megan. What's worse, Janelle kidnapped Megan's baby grandson. I think she'd do almost anything for money or revenge."

"And you and I could be suspects if we left, couldn't we?" she asked. "It would look like we just came here at Janelle's behest to cause more trouble for the Maitlands."

"Does that mean you're staying?"

"I can't leave without trying to repay Megan, anyway."

Rafe opened his mouth.

Laura shook her head. "On my own, Rafe, but thank you for almost offering. I have to do this on my own. No help."

He frowned at her. "If you'd let me help yesterday, you wouldn't have needed a rogue construction worker helping you. He didn't see you naked, did he, hon?"

Laura put on her best indignant older-sister look, even though she felt a blush creeping up. "It wasn't like that, Rafe. Believe me, the man wasn't thinking about anything improper at the time."

At that, he looked like he was going to argue. She shook her head and smiled, trying to distract him by making plans to meet his wife and maybe their half siblings, R.J. and Anna, her father's other family that she hadn't even known of until now.

After Rafe had gone, Laura cuddled Meggie close. "Just you and me, sweetie," she crooned.

And the scent of her baby made her recall a man with fierce, lake-blue eyes. A man who had, as Rafe implied, seen parts of her body and her soul that no one usually ever saw.

For half a second she allowed herself to wonder what Mick Hannon was doing right now.

Chapter Three

Eight days had gone by since Mick's debut as a labor coach, but right now he felt as tense as he had then. He rapped hard on the door Mrs. Parker had directed him to in her boardinghouse, hoping that Laura was home.

"Answer the door, hon," he said, raising his clenched fist to knock again.

Just then the door swung back and there she was, all green eyes and long bare legs beneath those denim cutoffs she was wearing. His breath nearly died in his throat. He'd forgotten what a lovely creature she was.

"Mick?" A trace of pink tinged her cheeks, and her voice rose as if she hadn't seen him in eight years instead of eight days. If things had worked out, that might well have been true, but things had happened and he couldn't stay away.

"Invite me in," he suggested with a lazy smile as

she stood there staring at him, her lovely lips parted slightly.

The sweet pink flush deepened. She smiled somewhat self-consciously. "Of course. Come in," she said, holding out her arm in a big swoop. "You startled me," she said by way of explanation.

No surprise. He'd startled himself by coming here.

"Where's your little munchkin?" he asked, looking around the room. Then he spied her bassinet in the corner. "Is she sleeping?" He lowered his voice to a whisper.

Just then a tiny pair of toes kicked into the air.

Laura chuckled. "I'd say…no. But she's happy right now. We can talk. Or maybe you just came to see the baby."

Confusion colored those green eyes. For a second Mick wondered how many men had lost track of their conversations just by staring into those eyes. He wondered how many men had forgotten to breathe just being this close to the soap-and-water-and-woman scent of Laura. He didn't kid himself into believing that he was the first whose chest felt tight when he looked at her. Meggie had been conceived by a man making love to Laura. A man who'd been so driven by passion that he'd failed to take precautions to protect her when he clearly hadn't wanted a child.

It wasn't a picture that he wanted to focus on, so he charged ahead with the subject that had drawn him here.

"I hear you're planning on working at the day-care center at the clinic," he began quietly.

Laura blinked. "My, word does spread quickly. I

only made that decision yesterday, but yes, I'll be starting in about a week. Why do you ask?''

He shrugged. ''I work outside the hospital, and gossip about the Maitlands spreads quickly. I know your daughter's name, that you have two brothers named Rafe and Luke, that you have half siblings named R.J. and Anna that you've just met for the first time in your life. I'm privy to all the news. That's why I'm here.''

He paused to look around before continuing. ''The clinic has experienced some acts of vandalism lately.''

''I know that.''

''It might be the Maitlands and not just the clinic that's being targeted.'' Mick spoke gently.

Her eyes widened. She sucked in a deep breath. ''You think I have something to do with what's been happening.''

Instantly he felt like giving himself a kick in the butt. ''Damn it, don't look like that. Of course I don't think that.''

She raised one brow. ''Why not? You don't know me.''

''You think I could stare into your eyes for hours and not know you a little?'' Ah, she didn't like that much better than she'd liked his first statement. The lady didn't want her privacy breached. Well, he understood that feeling all too well.

''Lady, I saw you with your baby, and I heard the way you spoke to me and to Megan. You wouldn't do anything to jeopardize her or any of the babies being born in that clinic.''

''I wouldn't,'' she said solemnly. ''And I thank you for saying that.''

Mick sighed. He had a feeling she didn't completely believe his words could be trusted. And maybe they couldn't, because there was a lot he wasn't telling her. Like the fact that it was his stepfather, Clyde Mitchum, who had deserted a pregnant Megan years ago. And the fact that Clyde was back in town and Mick had followed him here to keep an eye on him. And there was also the fact that he wasn't revealing that last little bit of information to anyone, least of all to Clyde.

No one knew that he and Clyde were related and no one would until he found out just what Clyde was up to, and he was definitely up to something, good or bad. He'd hinted as much on the phone a few weeks ago. But if Mick showed his hand now, he'd never know just what Clyde's plans were. His stepfather was more than capable of going underground.

"Laura, I'm concerned for you," he said, which was the absolute truth. "The clinic might not be a safe place. If you need a job, I'm sure I could find you one."

That delicate brow rose again. That delicate sexy brow. She was probably wondering just what kind of pull a construction worker would have. He was probably not going to tell her that he was on the verge of becoming a partner in Dell Douglas Construction at Dell's request, and that Dell knew most of the people in the Austin construction scene. It was how Mick had gotten this job, but saying that would lead to too many other explanations.

"You don't have to work at the clinic," he repeated.

She smiled. "I know. I have a brother who would

take me in if I'd let him. But I want this job. It will give me a chance to start to pay back Megan. They're short on employees at the day-care center and that means fewer employees at the clinic can leave their children there, and more absenteeism at the clinic itself. I could be a help. I love children, and I've studied nursing. I know enough to be of aid in an emergency.''

Okay, so there was going to be no talking her out of this. He tried to think fast.

''I'm going to worry about you, you know.'' His voice dropped soft and low and he found that he was only speaking the truth this time. It was going to drive him nuts not knowing when something was going to happen next, or even if something *was* going to happen next. He wished he knew just who had it in for the Maitlands so badly.

''You're such a good man, Mick.''

No, he was a heel. Here today, gone tomorrow, just like his alcoholic father had been and like Clyde was most of the time. And he could see that he wasn't making his point.

''You're determined to take this job?''

Her chin came up. ''I'm an adult, Mick. I make my own decisions.''

''I respect that, but it doesn't make me worry less. Will you do me a favor?''

''What kind of a favor?''

''Ease my mind. Let me at least see you to and from work. Let me stop in to check up on you now and then.''

''That's really not necessary.''

''You'd let me suffer when I don't have to?''

She grinned. "That's low, Mick."

He grinned back. "You bet it is, but it's also the truth. I'm not asking for the world."

She gazed down at her hands, which were resting in her lap. He was helpless not to look beyond her fingertips to that long bare stretch of legs. Mick took a deep breath and concentrated on the shiny crest of her hair.

"Laura?" he urged.

She brought her head up, her long hair swishing over her shoulders. "You stayed with me for hours. You didn't ask for anything, really, but letting you stand guard over me seems so…nineteenth century. I can take care of myself."

"Are your brothers capable of taking care of themselves?"

"Of course. They're grown men."

"Don't you worry about them now and then?"

"Every day. Especially Luke. I don't even know where he is."

"So it's okay to worry even if you trust them to be capable men."

She smiled at him and stood up, walking toward him. Her smile was both innocent and yet terribly dangerous to him. He wanted to reach out and touch, maybe even to grab. He forced himself to hold his hands still.

"You're too smart for your own good, Mick Hannon."

He shrugged. "That's not an answer."

"I don't see how letting you do something else for me would help in repaying you in any way."

"It would soothe me. It would help me concentrate. It's very important to concentrate when you're working with heavy machinery."

"Mick," she drawled. "Don't make me worry, too."

He got to his feet. He reached out and indulged himself by running one long finger down the smoothness of her cheek. "I'm a desperate man, Laura. I'm genuinely worried."

She nearly gasped at his touch, and a slight blush turned her cheeks an enticing, desirable rose. Skin made for nibbling on. Mick did his best to resist.

She frowned. "You shouldn't be worrying about me. That will only attract my brother's attention and then Rafe will be pacing the floor. You won't approach him?"

"Afraid it's too late. He approached me several days ago."

Laura frowned. "What did he want? No, don't tell me what he wanted. He didn't ask you if you—"

The rose of her cheeks had deepened. Mick couldn't resist. He leaned forward and touched his lips to her cheek, nibbled his way to her ear. "He asked me if I'd actually seen you naked."

She jumped, and he brought his arms up to catch her in case she should fall.

"What—what did you tell him?" she asked, and he knew that he'd be kissing her lips soon if he didn't step away. That wouldn't be a wise course for either of them, but especially for her. She was at a vulnerable stage of her life. He wasn't a man made for vulnerable women.

But he very definitely wanted to touch her again. He wanted to kiss more than just her cheek. And he wanted to do it in the dark in a bedroom.

He hesitated, then stepped away. "I told Rafe that the only thing I remember was your eyes. I was staring into your eyes the whole time."

She gazed up into his eyes then, and the room melted away.

"You were," she said, her voice low and soft and so terribly sexy that it was killing him. "I remember."

So did he. All too well.

"You'll let me be your temporary bodyguard, Laura?"

"Do you really think it's necessary?"

"Very necessary." It was a good thing she hadn't asked him if it was wise, because he knew for certain that getting too close to her wasn't wise at all. She made him feel big and protective, but he knew that wasn't a feeling that lasted with the men in his family. Inevitably they failed the women they had sworn to protect.

"What time do you start work?" he asked.

"I'm just part-time. They're letting me bring Meggie, of course. I begin at three and work until six."

"This late in the year, it'll be dark by the time you leave, then."

She nodded, so close that her swishing hair became trapped against his shoulder. He brushed his fingers through the soft silk and slid the strands back over her shoulder.

"Will you have any trouble getting off work to come pick me up?"

"It won't be any problem," he promised. "I have a very understanding supervisor." He did, but it wouldn't have mattered. Mick was determined to do whatever it took to protect Laura Maitland from whatever threatened her.

But as he took his leave and her soft scent wafted around him, he knew there was more at risk than he'd mentioned to her.

The lady was tempting as sin, and he had just set himself the task of seeing her several times a day. It was going to be one hell of a task to maintain some distance between Laura Maitland's lips and his own.

She definitely needed to do something about Mick Hannon, Laura thought a week later when Mick picked her up for work for the first time. It was all well and good to say that you were going to be assertive and independent, but with a man like Mick, a woman had to work very hard to stay a step ahead of him. He was a strong, stubborn man and he seemed to have a thing about protecting women.

"You really don't have to do this," she began, as Mick opened the door of his truck and fastened Meggie's carrier into the back seat.

He studied her for several seconds, a note of concern in his eyes. "Am I making you uncomfortable?" he finally asked.

She stared up at him, feeling small and delicate, even though her body still bore some of the evidence of her recent pregnancy.

Was he making her uncomfortable?

Definitely. The word stuck in her mind. What

woman wouldn't feel uncomfortable gazing up at a man who was a walking ad for how the human male should fill out his jeans? But the truth was that, nervous though that thought made her, there was also a certain comfort, a certain satisfaction in just being near the man.

An unexpected smile lifted her lips. "I feel just fine," she told him, lifting her chin in defiance.

A grin spread across his face, exposing even white teeth that contrasted sharply with his tanned skin. "That's good then, sunshine. Ready to ride?"

That low, sexy voice slid right under every womanly defense she'd spent months building.

Please don't let me be turning into my mother, she couldn't help thinking. Because Veronica Maitland had loved her husband even after he'd deserted her. Through all the long years after that, of working in bars and dating men with no future and trying her best to be a good mother, she'd still held out hope that Robert would return to her. If he whistled for her, she ran to him in a pant. If he called on the phone, she dropped everything. She was a sad, lonely woman, unable to enjoy life or even to enjoy her children that much, and Laura didn't ever intend to be like that. She'd allowed herself the mistake of hoping her father would love her. She'd even forgiven herself for thinking Greg was something he wasn't. But no more. She'd made her last big mistake with a man.

"This isn't going to work, you know," she said suddenly. "You escorting me to work doesn't count in the big book of *How Laura Pays Mick Back for Helping Her.*"

"It works for me."

She laughed, even though she wasn't feeling all that amused right now. She was sitting two feet away from a man who had a shadowed jawline made for stroking and a long, strong body made for satisfying a woman's needs.

"How can I expect Meggie to learn how to behave if I don't even show her the right way to thank someone?" she asked, forcing her thoughts back down the right lane.

Mick's laugh was low and seductive. "Um... Meggie would be how many days old now?"

Laura firmed her chin. "A parent should start the way they mean to go on."

Her comment brought a thoughtful smile to Mick's face. "You're an admirable woman, Laura," he said gently. "I'm sure you'll be one of the good parents. That's important."

His comment triggered a question in her mind. He sounded as if he had issues with parenting. She realized how little she knew about him. Maybe if she knew more, she'd know the right thing to do to demonstrate her gratitude. As it was, all she really knew was that he was handsome and that he was gallant. Well, okay, she *did* know that he worked in construction and was only here for the short term, but—

"Didn't you say you were just in from out of town?" she asked suddenly.

Instantly Mick's expression turned serious. He studied her carefully as if trying to decide what she was up to with this sudden change of subject. "Just in," he agreed quietly.

"Just here to do a job?"

"I'm here to do a job," he said.

Laura drummed her fingers lightly on the dashboard. The seeds of a plan—okay, the seeds of a very small plan—were building. Nothing great, but maybe more would come later.

"So…what do you usually do for supper?"

Mick turned curious eyes her way before looking back to the road. Suddenly he smiled.

"I usually eat," he teased.

"Where?"

He shrugged. "Fast food, a local diner, that kind of thing. Why?"

"No special reason. Just that you're away from home. Maybe you'd like food that was prepared just for you. Mrs. Parker has given me kitchen privileges if I want to have a guest rather than eat with all the other boarders. I could cook something for you. We could have a meal in my room, unless…"

"Unless?"

She felt her face burning. "I never thought. You don't have a wife who would get upset about another woman making you a meal, do you?"

In the silence that followed, the sound of the truck's engine filled her ears. Loudly.

"No wife," he finally said. "I'm not exactly marriage material."

His statement called for a question, but his tone told her he wasn't interested in answering questions.

"So would you be open to letting me work off my debt to you with food?"

"You don't have a debt."

She shook her head. "I have a bodyguard. I don't think most bodyguards work for free. Or at least they shouldn't."

Mick pulled up in front of the clinic. He cut the engine and turned dark, intense eyes her way, his arm looped over the steering wheel. Now that he wasn't driving, Laura was even more aware that he was an attractive, unmarried man...and that he was very close.

As if to punctuate that point, Mick leaned even closer. "Laura," he said softly. "I don't know how to say this tactfully, but I'm not sure it's wise for us to spend too much time alone in your room."

She sat there quietly chewing on her bottom lip, horribly embarrassed that he must have known what she had been thinking.

A low groan slipped from his lips. "Don't do that," he whispered, brushing her lip with his fingertips. And at that point of contact, she knew that he was right. It would be very dangerous for her to bring him into the private confines of her room at the boardinghouse. She'd be in much more danger than she probably ever would be in at the clinic, even with some sort of criminal harassing the Maitlands.

But an independent, modern woman wouldn't be that weak. Wasn't that what she was—or at least what she intended to become? If a woman wanted to be strong and assertive, darn it, she ought to take a firm stand in that direction.

Deliberately she turned to him, staring directly into his eyes. "I'm offering to cook for you, not bite your neck,'' she promised, fighting to keep herself from thinking about her words, hoping she wasn't blushing.

He still didn't answer, just sat there watching her. He opened his mouth as if to protest and she leaned closer.

''If I were a man, you'd let me repay my debts without protesting.''

He grinned then, finally, a great, sexy grin. ''Angel, no one on earth would mistake you for a man. And most, I might add, would be begging you to bite their necks, or they'd be trying to nibble on yours.''

''You're just trying to change the subject.''

''You've got me there. I don't feel comfortable letting a woman wait on me hand and foot.'' He didn't elaborate on that point. She wouldn't ask what he meant, since it was clearly personal.

But she had just about had enough.

''Okay, you've driven me to desperate measures. I *dare* you to taste my cooking,'' she said, looking down her nose as best she could and putting on the most superior smile she could manage when sitting next to a man who towered over her. ''If my cooking kills you, I promise I'll give you a proper burial, hard hat and all.'' She tossed off that last with an airy shake of her head, then crossed her arms.

''You think I'm a man who can't resist a dare?''

''Actually, I think you probably could, but I'm truly a desperate woman on this one issue. It was worth a try,'' she teased. ''Now I guess I'll be reduced to begging.''

All traces of humor fled Mick's face. ''Don't.''

''Don't what?''

"Don't humiliate yourself that way. I'll come to supper."

She studied him seriously. "I was teasing, Mick. I have too much pride for that."

The hollow look receded from his eyes slightly. "But you really want me to do this, don't you?"

"It's a matter of pride," she said softly.

He gazed into her eyes. "Pride's important. Don't ever let anyone steal that from you. Not for any reason. I'll come and have supper with you."

She smiled at him then and began to gather her purse and Meggie's things, but as she exited the truck, she found Mick at her side. "Laura?"

She looked up, a question in her eyes.

"Thank you," he said quietly.

But she wasn't sure whether he was thanking her for offering him a meal or for agreeing not to humble herself before him. No question, Mick was a complicated man.

Right now her life didn't need any more complications, especially none that were emanating from a man.

"Better save those thanks until you've tasted my cooking," she warned, choosing to make light of the matter. "I like to experiment with new things."

"Well," he said, "I guess that goes with the program where you're concerned, Laura. Every minute I'm with you, looks like I'm experimenting with new things. Childbirth, babies. Why should your cooking be any different?"

Laura didn't know. She only knew that everything about being with Mick seemed to be new for her, too.

That made it scary. "New" meant not knowing quite how to deal with the situation.

"Maybe we should stick to something safe tonight," she said suddenly.

Mick shook his head and laughed as he opened his door and climbed out of the truck to come around and help her with Meggie. "I think that's very good advice," he agreed. "Let's stick to something safe."

Laura was still mulling over his words as they neared the clinic's automatic doors. She turned to thank Mick for giving up his stubbornness and being a good sport, but as she pivoted, she noticed he had stopped five steps behind her.

"You'll be all right now," he said quietly. "I see Megan and Hugh, the clinic's attorney, just ahead. Don't forget that I'll be back for you after work."

She smiled. "Don't forget to build up an appetite."

His eyes turned dark and fierce. "That won't be a problem," he said. Then he was gone, loping toward a group of men in work boots and jeans.

She was alone as she entered the clinic, but not for long. Megan came toward her with a smile, flanked by two elderly men. One, a distinguished clean-cut man in a charcoal-gray suit, smiled at her.

"Laura dear, I'd like you to meet Hugh Blake, the clinic's corporate attorney and a very dear friend," Megan said graciously. "And this is Clyde Mitchum. Clyde's visiting the area."

The name Clyde rang a distinct bell. Laura knew the name and what the man had done to Megan.

Clyde nodded a polite but very brief greeting to Laura, immediately turning eager eyes back to Megan, as if he were afraid she'd slip away if he let her out of his sight. Laura wondered what that was about, but she didn't have long to ponder the subject.

"It's a pleasure to meet you, Laura," Hugh said as she murmured her hello. "You're the woman we've all heard about, the one with the beautiful baby, isn't she, Megan?" Hugh held out his hand to Laura. He squatted down and ran a gentle hand over Meggie's head, and his eyes glowed when he looked up at Megan. "She really is a beauty, my dear. Just as you said," he whispered reverently. "And to think, you had a hand in her birth."

"Not much. Mostly I talked while everyone else worked. Besides, just being there was an honor," Megan said. "I don't get to do much more than paperwork usually."

"Nonsense," Hugh said vehemently, rising to his feet. "You've made Maitland Maternity a haven. Without you, there'd be no place for many women to get this kind of care. You're the imagination and the brains behind the clinic."

"You're a first-rate spokeswoman, too," Clyde added, nodding at Megan.

Hugh frowned slightly at the man. "She's the very best," he added.

"You've really worked some miracles here, Meg," Clyde said. "Your children have all grown into real winners, your clinic is a hell of a fine place." The man's voice sounded earnest, but Laura couldn't forget what he'd once done to Megan.

Apparently Hugh couldn't, either. He looked distinctly uncomfortable with Clyde Mitchum's words.

"You're the greatest treasure this clinic has, Megan," he said softly.

Megan smiled at him and Laura thought she saw a soft glow in the woman's blue eyes. Then Megan turned toward Laura.

"Come on, Laura dear. We'd better go get you settled before my head gets too big to fit through the day-care center's door."

Laura chuckled and lifted her daughter's carrier higher in her arms. She smiled down at her baby.

"Come on, Meggie love, first day for both of us. Let's go get started."

She noted that Megan smiled politely at both Hugh and Clyde as she walked away from them, and Laura couldn't help wondering about Megan's relationship with these two men who obviously wanted her attention. Most especially she wondered about Clyde.

How could a woman ever forgive a man who'd knowingly betrayed her trust? And even if she managed to forgive, could she ever really take the next step and trust him with her heart again?

It didn't seem likely, but as Laura followed Megan to the day-care center, she knew that it really wasn't her concern. All she had to worry about today was a roomful of sweet little babies. All she had to worry about *tonight* was how to get through an evening with Mick Hannon without letting him know that she wanted to taste his skin.

Chapter Four

Mick couldn't exactly say that he'd ever been nervous in a woman's presence before. He'd always had his share of women wanting him to touch, and he'd done more than his fair share of touching. But he'd also always confined himself to women who were only interested in the pleasures of short-term companionship. He had his reasons, and he was mentally reciting them right now while he sat across from Laura Maitland and watched her slowly slip a spoonful of chocolate parfait between her pale pink lips.

He damn near groaned as he watched the delicacy slide out of sight, and it was all he could do not to reach across the table and drag her from her chair onto his lap.

Don't try it, Hannon, he warned himself. Laura wasn't the type of woman a man offered a short and blazing sexual relationship. She was the type a man could hurt too easily, and Mick had seen enough of men making a woman cry to last him a lifetime. He knew he could be charming, but he also knew too well that a man could be charming and could be charmed until he'd married and settled in. That was where the difficulties started.

Mick took one look at Laura's wide-eyed innocence as she withdrew the spoon from her mouth and realized that he was in one difficult situation right now. He wanted to linger over her lips a lot more than he wanted to eat.

"I'm sorry. You don't like chocolate?" she asked, noting the parfait he had yet to touch.

What was he supposed to say? That he'd been too busy savoring the erotic experience of watching her eat to even think about touching his own dessert? The very thought of revealing his thoughts made him grin.

"What?" she demanded.

He shook his head. "You make eating dessert an art," he confessed.

Immediately she looked slightly sheepish. "Dessert is my weakness. We almost never had it when I was a kid."

Neither had he. It was why he always made himself wait to eat it. But he could see that he was going to hurt her feelings if he waited any longer, so he picked up his spoon, dipped it in the chocolate cream and tasted.

It was heaven, the kind of thing a man wanted to dribble on a woman's naked body, then take several hours licking the sweetness from her skin.

"It's great," he said carefully, and she primly nodded her thanks.

"You have any more?" he added, and her prim nod turned into a glowing smile. As she moved to the small table where she'd left the extras, he noted for the nineteenth time tonight how quickly she'd turned this room into as much of a home as she could. Small touches of rose-and-plum table runners, pink flowers, a shallow bowl with wine-colored candles floating amid white blossoms—all turned what would otherwise have been a stark room decorated in an overabundance of green into something much more.

A small blue ceramic angel with gilded white wings sat on a table. Cracks where it had been mended were visible. Following the direction of his gaze, Laura walked over and picked it up.

"I know it's gaudy, but it was my mother's. She was a Vegas showgirl, and I think the angel reminded her that she'd once been an innocent, loving little girl. When I fell outside the clinic, I dropped my bag and broke her. It's a silly thing to keep, anyway, I guess. She was a silly woman." Her tone told him she didn't want to pursue the subject.

He couldn't help thinking that Laura was a little like the angel, resilient yet eminently breakable. It was pretty clear she wouldn't want to think of herself as fragile, though.

"You've only been here a little over a week, but you've made yourself a home and a special space for Meggie." He nodded toward the quilted alphabet hangings surrounding her bassinet.

"I wanted her to have things around her that would make her happy."

Which only confirmed his suspicions that Laura was

a caring mother who would one day get over her hurt and want a stable man to father her child. They'd be lining up by the thousands to interview for the position, too.

He veered away from the vision of hot-eyed men doing their best to please Laura. He felt a need to move.

"Let me help you with those," he said as she began to put the empty dishes on a tray to carry downstairs.

She started to open her mouth. To protest, he could tell.

He smiled. "If I don't lead by example, how will Meggie know that doing dishes is a man's job as well as a woman's?"

Laura's low laugh was a gift as she accepted his help. Mick swept up the crumbs. She stacked the glasses. They worked side by side, but in the small confines of the room, their elbows bumped.

"Rats," Laura said with a chuckle, as she bobbled a glass. She lunged, her hand missing the glass by a good six inches.

Mick dropped down and scooped the glass up only inches from the floor. Carefully, he set it down on the floor, then looked up at the woman he was now kneeling before.

Only inches separated their bodies. If he leaned forward slightly, he could touch his lips to the soft pink of her blouse. He could feel her warm skin tremble beneath the cloth.

Heat ripped through him, as he forced his silent urgings away and ordered himself to get to his feet. He tried to control the hunger churning within him as his body slid past hers when he stood.

The scent of lilacs drifted to him, and he wondered if it came from her hair—or from her skin. The need to move close enough to find out was intense, but he did his best to hold himself still.

"Thank you," she whispered, and the hushed tone of her voice slithered through him and shattered his good intentions.

That was all it took. Her voice. Two words, low, quiet, her breath wafting over his skin like a runaway kiss. He groaned and leaned toward her, and then she was in his arms, the silk of her hair sliding against his chest, her fragrance driving him crazy, her softer-than-flower-petals skin driving him even crazier.

He wanted more of her. He wanted her taste in his mouth, her lips opening in surrender.

Slowly he drew her closer, closer still, until the tips of her breasts brushed his chest, and a tiny gasp escaped her. She froze then, and looked straight up into his eyes.

He saw it then more clearly, that he was not alone in this madness. He could kiss her if he wanted to. He could kiss her more than once.

She parted her lips to speak and he swooped in slowly, very slowly. She was trembling, and he realized just how small she was, how alone. He should let her go, end this thing now. Neither of them appeared to be in control of…anything. Still, he was close, so close. His entire body was vibrating with the tension of holding himself at bay. His mouth was the merest breath away from hers.

Desire fought with reason. Need made him want to surge forward. Only the thinnest sliver of responsibility kept him from closing the distance between his body and hers.

"Mick?" Laura asked as he hesitated, her lips moving so close beneath his that he stopped breathing for half a second. The mere act of speaking brought her closer against him.

"Hell," he muttered beneath his breath, and she opened her mouth again.

"No. Don't say anything," he urged, pulling back slightly. "If we—if we don't move for a second or two, I can get on top of this thing. I can stop myself from taking this where you really don't want me to go."

She held herself still.

And then she didn't.

Like a swift butterfly aiming for a flower, she rose on her toes and touched her lips to his. He breathed her in, he savored the tingle of her skin barely hovering on his, and then his mind short-circuited. Reason fled. He slid his arm behind her back and touched her fully, bringing her in toward his body. He took possession of her, covering her mouth with his own. He feasted.

She tasted exotic, a combination of chocolate and flowers and something that was her own sweet flavor. She tasted better than chocolate parfaits made with magic.

For whole seconds he savored her, relishing her tiny movements as she slid more closely into his embrace. He sampled the delicate skin just inside her lips and was rewarded with a sigh. The sensation of her fingers pressing lightly against his chest sent pleasure spiraling through him.

He reached down to cover her hand with his own.

That single movement did it. It was as if the ceramic angel on the table had spoken. It was as if time spun back several days to those hours when their fingers had twined so desperately.

He remembered once again that she was a vulnerable woman who had to have had some unfortunate dealings with a man, and that he was a man who wanted to avoid any unfortunate dealings with a woman. This moment wasn't meant to be, this moment was a mishap. Any man who took advantage of this accident would be...lucky, but he'd also be the worst kind of man, one who took advantage of a woman who was still struggling with the emotional upheaval of starting a new life in a new place with a new baby.

She apparently remembered something, too, because her body stiffened, and she pulled back to stare up at him, her eyes slightly scared.

"I can't believe I did that," she said slowly as he helped her gain her balance and they stepped away from each other, letting the cool air fill in the space between their bodies.

"I'm pretty sure there was a 'we' involved," he said gently, daring the fates as he tucked his finger beneath her chin. "My body was definitely involved in the process."

"But I was the one who started it."

He gave a low chuckle. "No, I think this was something that started days ago. We're just now catching up with all the sensations that have been swirling around us."

She nodded tightly. "I can't do this, Mick."

His smile was slow and sad. "I wouldn't let you. I'm not what you need."

"I don't need anyone. Except Meggie."

He nodded, even though he still doubted that her statement would hold true forever. For now she was hurt, but someday she would need someone. It just wouldn't and couldn't be him.

The ringing of the phone brought the room into sudden clarity. He thanked the gods and Mrs. Parker for installing the darn thing.

Laura picked up the receiver. "Rafe? What? The television? Yes, there's one downstairs if it's not being used. All right. Yes, I will."

She hung up, a confused look in her eyes. "Rafe says that the local station is running teasers on some report *Tattle Today TV* is doing and that I should probably watch it. It's something about the clinic, but...well, this isn't my house. I can't just barge in and insist on watching whatever I want to watch."

He smiled at her concern about the other boarders. Right now there weren't a great many, and most of those were men. A couple were even fellow workers of his. Getting control of the remote wouldn't be a problem when he showed up downstairs with the best-looking woman in the area who just happened to need a small favor. Automatically, Mick walked over to the bassinet, giving Meggie a good look for the first time. He'd carefully rationed his glimpses during the few times he'd spent with Laura and Meggie.

Big blue eyes gazed back at him, small baby noises came from her.

"You can pick her up. She won't bite. No teeth."

He wanted to smile, and yet he didn't. Instead, he looked up at Laura. "I might hurt such a little thing."

Laura shook her head. "You're a gentle man. You just need to support her head and hold her close and she'll be fine."

Support. Closeness. Nothing he was good at or wanted to start yearning for.

"Better bring her with us if we're going downstairs," he whispered, but he didn't pick the baby up.

Laura nodded and lifted her child into her arms.

"Let's go take possession of the television," he said, holding out his hand. "No need for you to worry about stepping on toes. I'll take care of things." Babies he couldn't handle. This he could.

She placed her hand in his, and he ignored the urge to tug her closer. Instead he moved to the door, which she opened. He led the way down the stairs. Halfway down, the sound of the television reached them. A commercial was just ending. Blossom Woodward, reporter for *Tattle Today TV,* filled the screen, her blond beauty mesmerizing.

Then Mick froze and Laura bumped up against his shoulder softly. Automatically, she shielded her baby from hurt.

Laura's face appeared on the screen.

"Another incident in the strange series of incidents at the Maitland Maternity clinic took place today," Blossom was saying. "A security camera in the east wing was vandalized, its tape removed, and hours of information has gone missing. Another incident like several that have taken place at Maitland Maternity in the past few weeks. Only this time there are even more interesting issues that have been raised, because just today, Laura Maitland came on board as an employee of the Maitland Maternity clinic's day-care center. An intriguing and puzzling situation, given the fact that Janelle Maitland, Laura Maitland's sister, is the same woman who recently kidnapped a Maitland baby. One can only wonder what Megan Maitland, CEO of the clinic, R.J. Maitland, president of the clinic, and Beth Maitland, manager of the day-care center, were thinking when they made the decision to hire this young woman.''

But it was obvious what everyone in the downstairs room of the boardinghouse was thinking. All eyes turned from the television toward Laura as the piece ended and the rest of the news scrolled on. Someone turned off the set. Silence filled the room like noxious gas. No questions were asked, but they were there, written in the five pairs of eyes focused on Laura.

Automatically, Mick pulled Laura closer to his side. No one, not anyone here or elsewhere, was going to ask her one single question, not while he was around.

That didn't mean that tons of questions weren't barreling through his own mind. Who in hell had it in for Maitland Maternity? Was someone trying to hurt Laura or just trying to hide behind her convenient presence? And what was Clyde up to? He'd been terribly affected by the death of Mick's mother, Maeve. Was he here to turn over a new leaf or here to try to take advantage of the fact that he'd just realized he was connected to the wealthy Maitlands through his newly discovered son?

An even better question was why he himself wasn't keeping better tabs on his stepfather.

But he knew the answer to that. He'd been keeping an eye on Laura, and Laura was a great deal more distracting than Clyde.

At that moment, she was carefully extricating herself from his grasp and moving the rest of the way down the stairs.

"Laura," he said carefully. She stopped and turned, and he took advantage of her temporary halt. He moved beyond her into the room where the sea of faces waited to see what would happen with their suddenly notorious fellow boarder.

"Boys, I think it's time to turn the television off and find something else to do, don't you?" he asked quietly. He met their gazes head on, daring them to say one word to the lady behind him.

Except...she was here, stepping away from the protection he was trying to give her. "Thank you, Mick," she said softly, "but people have a right to wonder. Though I have spoken to the police and I wasn't even in town when the first incident happened. The police think I'm innocent but obviously the media is harder to convince. Mrs. Parker," she said to the woman in the corner whose knitting now sat ignored in her lap. "I think it's time I started to look for a place of my own. It's only fair to you."

"Oh, now, dear, you don't have to do that," the woman said. "I've been in this business a very long time, and I know an honest person when I see one."

"And I want you to stay in the business for even longer," Laura answered. "Besides, with all the hoopla, people might decide Meggie and I are a curiosity. They'll be knocking on your door all the time. What kind of a mother would I be if I didn't try to find a private place to protect my child from curious eyes?"

Mick's throat felt tight. She'd obviously be a good mother no matter what.

"Laura?" he asked gently, and he reached out and touched her hand, which rested on the baby's back.

She shook her head. "I'm all right. I'm fine," she said.

But she wasn't. Her voice was calm, but her hand was ice cold and trembling.

A fierce sense of protectiveness washed over him. A need to pull her close, even though he couldn't with all these people gathered around. Already she had people talking about her. She didn't need him to be causing her any more grief.

The thought that he and his family might be the ones causing her grief in the first place didn't escape him.

He hoped it wasn't so, but if it were...would she ever forgive him?

And would he forgive himself?

"Let's get you out of here. Now," he said.

Chapter Five

They had barely retreated to her room and settled Meggie into her bassinet when the phone rang. Caught off guard, Laura tensed. She stared at the phone, but she didn't reach for it. The television had been bad enough. Now the reactions would begin, and there were plenty of people who would know how and where to find her. The clinic was a gossipy place, and Mrs. Parker's boardinghouse was well known.

Mick let out a growl and stalked over to the phone. He reached for the line connecting it to the wall.

Laura put out her hand. "No, it might be Rafe. He'll be worried. He'll be even more worried if he can't reach me."

"You're sure?" She knew what he meant. Having grown up with a mother who was a showgirl, she knew all too well that there were people who could be callous and crude in both the things they thought and the things they said. There had always been plenty who were willing to offer her their opinion on her mother's morals. That person on the other end of the line might just be waiting to accuse her of…anything. If she picked up the phone, she was risking abuse. But she'd already worried her brother enough. If Rafe had heard the television report, he would be going mad.

"I'm sure," she said as the phone rang yet again.

He nodded solemnly, his mouth a thin line. "If it's not Rafe, give the phone to me."

And then he'd be fighting her battles. It just wasn't going to happen, but she avoided that issue by reaching for the phone. With the greatest of effort, she kept her hand from shaking so that Mick couldn't see how daunting this was.

"Laura?"

It wasn't Rafe, and it wasn't your garden-variety abusive phone call, either. It was Megan. Laura worked to find her voice.

"You saw," Laura said simply, quietly.

"Yes."

"I'll find other work, of course. Believe me, I understand."

A long hesitation followed. "I'm afraid you understand wrong, then. I hired you, Laura. It's my decision whether I want to fire you or not. Not the media's."

Laura glanced at Mick, who was shifting from one foot to the other. The man looked as if he wanted to put his fist through the wall. He looked as if he still might tug the phone line right out of the machine.

She wished she could soothe him, but she was incapable of such an action right now.

"Megan, I've heard of all the things that have been

going on at the clinic. After Janelle, it has to have crossed your mind that I might be the culprit.''

"Are you?''

Laura took a deep, shaky breath. Mick moved closer, a question in his eyes. ''No,'' she said, to both Megan and Mick.

"Then there's no problem.'' Megan's voice was gentle and sad. Laura remembered all the bad things that had happened to the woman over the years, from being abandoned by Clyde Mitchum to being told that her child had died and having it adopted by another family, to having her grandson kidnapped after she'd finally been reunited with her son. After all of that, how could she not be more cautious? Indignation rose up in Laura, a determination to protect Megan from possible hurt.

"Megan, anyone would ask me to leave after today. The evidence is too damning. I'm Janelle's sister.''

"You don't want the job?''

She wanted it desperately. Moreover, she needed it, but she didn't want to live under a cloud or raise her baby under that same dark cloud. Her own childhood had been like that.

"I love the job,'' she said sincerely, ''but—''

"Good,'' Megan said in that calming voice. ''Because I called to let you know that if you decide to stay, you'll do so with my backing and my protection. I'm not naive, Laura. I know the facts, and yes, you could be lying to me, but family has to mean something. It means everything to me. I have to believe that my family has honor and integrity. You're a member of my family, even though we've just met. What's more, you were very upfront about telling me who you were and why you were here. You could be lying about all of that. I've obviously been burned before, but…a person has to gamble now and then on the things she believes in. I'm choosing to believe that you're an honorable woman. No, I know you're an honorable woman.''

Laura looked up to find that Mick had moved closer to her, as if he could protect her with his body from whatever words were pouring through the telephone wires. It was a comforting thought. For that second, with Megan reassuring her on one end of the line and Mick hovering near on the other, she felt such warm gratitude that her eyes were in danger of tearing up. She blinked rapidly and Mick frowned.

She shook her head. "How can you be sure?" she asked Megan, her voice coming out a bit softer than she might have liked.

Megan's laughter was low and light. "My dear, you and I spent some of the most personal hours two women can share. Mick and I talked you through childbirth, a process that brings out the best or the worst in a woman. It brought out the best in you. Even in your pain, you worried about others. You cared about your child, too. And I saw you in the day-care center today. If I thought for one millisecond that you would endanger one of those children, I'd drop you in a heartbeat no matter who you were. But what I saw was a woman who delights in the laughter of children, who cuddles them even when their faces are dirty, who adores them. And I challenge anyone to say that you're not the right woman for the job.''

Laura's eyes did fill with tears then. She had loved her mother and pitied her. She had mourned her and missed her. Megan was not the mother she had lost and never would be, but she was a woman Laura couldn't help admiring and caring about.

"Thank you. I won't fail you."

As she hung up the phone, it rang again. Automatically, she picked it up. The words that came at her were foul, ugly and threatening. She dropped the receiver as if it were a hand grenade. It bounced off the floor with a clatter.

Mick picked it up and put it to his ear though she tried to stop him.

"No one there," he said tersely. "Mind if I ask who it was?"

And what would he do if she told him? He would be dead set on fixing things for her. She could see that in the ice blue of his eyes.

"Wrong number," she said. "The first one was Megan. She told me to be at work on time tomorrow."

Her smile was as genuine as she could manage. Mick's lips almost turned up enough to be called a smile, but then he started looking around the room. He eyed the couch with interest.

"Got an extra pillow?"

She swallowed hard. "Why?" she managed to choke out.

When he turned back, his eyes were more gentle, his jaw less tense. "It's late. I thought I might stay tonight. Just in case you need me." He glanced toward the phone.

The thought of him staying here to protect her from

the harsh phone calls and anyone who might finally take it into his head to come bang on the door made her heart turn warm with yearning.

And there she'd be, a carbon copy of Veronica Maitland.

"I have lots of locks," she pointed out, nodding toward the door. "And I know how to hang up the phone. It's a skill my mother taught me."

"Laura," he drawled, as if he might convince her just by using that tone. And there was the danger. If she listened to that velvet, masculine voice that dragged at her senses, he might convince her of anything. Then she *would* be her mother all over again.

Slowly she shook her head. "I'm very grateful, but I really need to get through this on my own. It's important. I came to this town, meaning to make a fresh start. I have to do that all by myself."

"I understand, but I don't believe you were expecting to be thrown into the Maitland clinic's controversy when you arrived."

"No, I didn't. Nevertheless..." She twisted her hands together nervously.

He reached out and untwined her fingers, taking her hands in his own. "All right, I won't press you. You have enough to think about without a boneheaded man pestering you. I'll check on you in the morning."

And he leaned down and kissed her just beneath her jawline, right where a frantic pulse was fluttering.

She swallowed hard and resisted the urge to lean close and ask him to kiss her again. On her lips this time.

Once he had gone, she slid home the locks, then

slipped down the wall to the floor. He was right about one thing. When she'd come to Austin, she hadn't expected to become the media's suspect in the acts of vandalism.

And she certainly hadn't expected Mick Hannon. Sending him home had been an act of courage, but it was a futile act, after all. He would show up in her dreams later tonight. And tomorrow?

Well, he said he'd be back. She tried to stem the sense of anticipation she was feeling and failed miserably.

Laura circled another apartment ad in the Austin *American-Statesman* just as a pounding sounded on her door. Automatically, she went to answer it, then hesitated. After last night's announcement and some of the angry phone calls that had followed, she had to be more careful. Especially now that she had Meggie to think of.

Carefully, she slipped the chain on the door, then opened it a notch.

Serious blue eyes stared down at her. Mick gave her a quick nod. "I'm glad you're being smart about safety. Mind if I come in?"

Laura blinked. It was only nine in the morning, much too early for her to be going to work. In fact, Mick should probably be at work right now.

She undid the chain and stepped aside. "What's wrong?" she asked, her voice not much more than a whisper.

He didn't answer. Instead, he glanced toward the phone and saw that it was disconnected.

"That's what I thought. People have been bothering you, haven't they?"

She shrugged. "People love the Maitlands, Mick. Understandably so. They want to make sure they're not in any danger."

"They scared you enough that you had to finally disconnect your phone, after all."

"Not really," she lied, noting the traces of sleeplessness on his face. The same signs she'd noted in her own mirror this morning. "I just didn't want them to keep waking Meggie. Besides, not all of the calls were bad. Rafe wants me to move in with him and Greer."

"That's a wise idea," he said, his voice gentle. He reached out and tucked a loose strand of hair behind her ear. She realized that she was still in her thin blue bathrobe and that her hair had yet to be tamed.

Laura shook her head. "It's a terrible idea. My brother and his wife have just gotten married. They need privacy. I'm not going there."

"And you're not staying here? Where then? Laura, I don't want to wound your pride in any way, but I want to help. It's why I'm here."

She smiled then. She wasn't going to tell him that Megan Maitland had also called back and offered to help. A distinct sense of unease shifted within her. She seemed to remember declaring that she'd come to Maitland Maternity because she didn't have enough money to go elsewhere. Megan and Mick would have remembered that. Something deep and warm blossomed within her. She looked up at the beautiful male who was shifting in front of her. She'd just bet that he was trying to think of some way of offering her money without damaging her pride.

She gently placed a hand on his arm. "I'm only working part-time right now, but Megan's paying me more than she should. And I do have a little bit of money saved, enough so that I can afford a small place for Meggie and me."

Mick's skin was warm through the thin cotton of his shirt. He looked down into her eyes and she thought for a moment that he was going to protest. Then he shrugged. "Need help finding a place?"

His voice was low, slightly husky. For a moment, she very much wanted to say *yes.* Anticipation at the thought of sharing long hours listening to Mick's voice, smiling into those mesmerizing blue eyes, being close enough to touch, rose within her. Which was the very reason she shook her head.

"Pick me up for work. That was the deal," she said.

"You don't have to work today?"

He grinned then. "I have an understanding employer," he said once again.

She didn't grin back. This was beginning to sound…wrong. Or maybe it was just natural for her to suspect every man's words. She nodded slowly.

"You must have a *very* understanding employer."

"You're sure you'll be all right today?" he asked, skirting the question in her tone. And she knew that he had begged the day off work because he was worried about her. Tears formed at the backs of her eyes. She fought to keep them there so that he wouldn't see.

"By the time you see me again today, I intend to

have a new place to call home. I'll be perfectly fine. I'm used to landing on my feet.''

A slight frown marred his forehead at her comment, but he nodded. ''Be careful,'' he said, his voice rough.

''I'm the most careful woman you'll ever meet.''

''Good. Keep it that way.'' And he left her to do her apartment-hunting alone.

She got out a bus schedule and the number of a cab company just in case she needed it. She thought of the small bit of cash she had available and hoped she could find some place that wouldn't make alarms go off in Mick's head. The man had a protective streak ten miles wide. If she couldn't afford something that looked at least safe, she had the feeling he was going to inject himself into her life more than was wise. And then she would never feel safe.

Mick Hannon made her want things she just wasn't going to allow herself to have.

Or maybe Mick Hannon just plain old made her want. And ache. Period. What the heck was she going to do about that?

Mick stared at the sad little blue garage with the tiny apartment above it, and then he looked at the lady standing by his side. Laura's green eyes were eager with delight, as if she'd just rented a castle. He suspected that she was just happy to have been able to find a place that she could afford. He was beginning to realize how important it was to her to be able to provide for her child. Without help. Without assistance from any man. His formerly pregnant beauty had a great deal of pride. He intended to make sure no one stole that from her.

"Well?" she asked, gazing up at him, her teeth biting softly into her lower lip. As he watched her, she swallowed nervously, her pulse dancing in her throat. He wanted to protect her. He wanted to place his lips over that pulse and breathe in her scent, taste her, have her.

He swallowed, almost as nervously as she had, even if his reasons were different.

"You work fast," he said, making sure he had a smile on his face when he said it. No way was he going to let his doubts show. As long as the door had locks and the neighborhood was safe enough, he was going to make sure she got credit for her achievement.

Laura chuckled. "Okay, I know it's nothing elegant or even mildly aesthetically pleasing, but it has a kitchen and a bathroom, double locks on the doors," she emphasized, grinning at him, "and it's furnished. It's closer to the clinic, too, so you won't have to drive me as far."

A strong sense of disappointment slipped through Mick. He forced it aside. "Shall we go inside?" It struck him that the apartment was probably very small, and since Meggie had been sleeping when they left the day-care center, they had left the child there while they took this short trip. He and Laura would be completely alone in this body-bumping space.

"Welcome to my palace," Laura said, holding up her key. She climbed the narrow steps that eased alongside the garage, her hips swaying gently just in front of Mick's eyes.

He dragged in a breath. When had he decided to become noble? And why, when he wanted nothing more than to reach out and slip his hands around Laura Maitland's hips and pull her soft body against his? But then she stopped, looking over her shoulder and smiling excitedly, like a child, and he remembered.

Laura, for all her new motherhood, was innocent and vulnerable and some creep of a man had hurt her badly and then left her. What's more, Mick Hannon wasn't a staying kind of man. If he took her, he would be the next creep in her life.

"Here we are," she said, inserting the key in the door, turning it and admitting them to her new home.

Mick followed her inside to the emptiest furnished twenty-by-twenty room he had ever seen. A kitchen counter with stools and cabinets took up one corner, a clean but overstuffed blue plaid couch sat under a window, and a narrow double bed filled another corner. That was all that had been provided.

Mick turned to look at Laura, his mind scrambling for the right words.

"I've lived in plenty of places with less," she said, her hands twisting around each other. "At least it's clean, and the landlord gave me a good deal. He's old and he has grown children in Chicago where he stays half the time. I suggested that if I agreed to watch his cars and his house, he wouldn't have to worry about thieves. He liked the idea enough to give me a break on the rent."

A surge of pure admiration poured through Mick's soul. He looked down at this delicate, lovely women who must have endured things in her life that he couldn't even imagine, and yet she still kept fighting for the freedom to live her life on her own terms.

With new eyes, he gazed around the small confines of the apartment. "It's clean," he agreed, "and it's cozy. It's a safe neighborhood, and…" He grinned. "I like the wallpaper. Kind of unusual."

Laura frowned. She looked more closely at what appeared to be simple cream-colored paper with green dots on it. On closer inspection, the truth came out.

She chuckled. "Frogs. My whole apartment is wall-papered in frogs? I think I like that."

She smiled up at him and Mick couldn't help reaching for her, snagging her by the waist and pulling her to him. He was pretty darn sure that he liked *her*. Too much. But still…

"Congratulations on your new home, Laura," he whispered. "When I'm back in Dallas, I'll think of you here. You and Meggie and your frogs."

And he kissed her. Slowly. So slowly. Lingering over her lips the way she'd lingered over her chocolate dessert. Tasting, savoring, drawing her in closer to him.

Her head fell back, exposing the cream of her throat to him.

He kissed her right there, on that wildly racing pulse point, and she moaned. She twined her hands into his hair, raised her head and kissed him back, full on the mouth. She moaned again, right into his mouth.

"This is almost the stupidest thing I've ever done," she whispered softly against his lips when they came up for air. He knew darn well that the "stupidest" thing she was referring to had something to do with that scum who had left her.

"We'll stop doing it soon," he promised, and kissed her again.

She nodded, her lips rubbing against his, making him ache. Then she pulled away, stepped away. "Yes," she agreed. "You'll be gone soon. Off to another work site."

And another woman, she was implying. He couldn't argue with her. Hadn't he always done that, been that way, just like his worthless father before him, just like Meggie's father?

"I don't want this to happen," she said, and he was wondering if she was warning him or talking to herself.

He gently cupped her face in his big hands and gazed earnestly into her green eyes. "I'm sorry," he said. "I shouldn't keep touching you like this."

She shook her head. "Don't be sorry. Just understand that I don't want to do this again. I can't. I have a child to think about this time."

His hands fell away. She was right. He was taking advantage. It was unacceptable, but wasn't it just like him? Hadn't he always known he would be a man to take advantage?

"You need furniture," he said, stepping away.

"Not much. I have a couch and a bed."

Mick eyed the thin brittle wood of the bedstead, the sagging narrow mattress.

"That's not a bed. You need furniture."

She got that stubborn set to her chin and he almost

leaned down and kissed her right there. Instead, he forced himself to be still. He managed to grin at her.

"I know a carpenter," he whispered. "He'll make you a bed. No charge."

Now her chin rose higher.

"Why would he do that?"

"He owes you."

Suspicion filled her eyes. "No one in this town owes me anything."

"No one in this town has gotten to taste your lips. Most men would pay a great deal to do that. I'm the only one. I owe you. I'll make you a bed."

"You won't. I don't want to be in debt to anyone, not for anything."

Mick took a deep breath. "You know I'm going to worry about you as long as I'm here." If he stayed near enough, maybe he could protect her from whoever was targeting the Maitlands, and maybe he could protect her from the gossips.

But she wasn't buying yet. She lifted her chin higher.

"You know I'm going to hover," he continued. "If I hover, I'll want to touch. I'll want to taste. I'll want to take. Making furniture will keep my hands busy, and both of us will be better off if my hands are occupied and off of you."

Her eyes had widened as he spoke. A lovely pink blush had climbed up her throat and suffused her face. She opened her mouth, but seemed unable to find words to say.

"I don't want you to put in extra work over me."

He leaned down closer, his lips a breath away from

hers. "I don't want to risk kissing you again, and I'm very near the edge, Laura. Do me a favor. Give me something useful to do with my time and with my hands. If my hands aren't near you, my lips won't be, either."

For five seconds they stood there together. He could almost taste her, they were that close. All she had to do was lean. All he had to do was reach. His hands itched to reach. She swayed slightly, bringing her body even closer.

He was pretty darn sure he was going to go out of his mind if he couldn't have her right now.

Then she closed her eyes.

"Just a bed," she agreed, pulling back.

He dragged in a deep breath and took a step back. He had what he wanted…or at least he had what he'd been aiming for. What he wanted was something else entirely.

"Just a bed," he said, his voice low and husky. Just a bed. For now.

He'd won them some time. For right now, he could keep his hands and his lips off her. That was good, even if it was only a temporary reprieve. And it was only temporary, because no question about it, as long as he was here in Austin, his nights were going to be spent dreaming hot dreams of Laura Maitland. He was going to want her every step of the way.

It was time to speed up his business here and find out what was up with Clyde. He wouldn't use her. He swore he wouldn't use her. But only by discovering the truth about Clyde could he truly help anyone and speed himself along and away from Austin, out of the reach of Laura and temptation.

It was time to get down to business. He would do that tonight. Right now he intended to make sure that last night's broadcast didn't have an effect on Laura's afternoon at the clinic.

Chapter Six

It was nearing six o'clock that evening when Laura looked up from putting a bandage on a toddler's imaginary boo-boo and saw Mick filling up the doorway of the day-care center. His blue-eyed gaze took in everything at once, her position on the floor, the child in front of her, the deepest corners of the room. He'd insisted on escorting her to the door this afternoon and now here he was again. Clearly in full bodyguard mode. An achingly broad-shouldered bodyguard, she couldn't help thinking with a weary smile as she rose to her feet.

He pasted on his own tight smile as she hugged the little boy and sent him on his way with a quick whisper of encouragement.

"Hi," she said softly to Mick as he uncrossed his arms and advanced on her.

He nodded. "Time to go, sunshine." His words were friendly, but the muscles beneath his black

T-shirt didn't relax even slightly as he moved farther into the room. "How was your day?"

It had been hell. Several parents upset with Blossom Woodward's report had pulled their children from the center in spite of Megan and Beth Maitland's reassurances.

"It was fine," she said quickly, knowing he'd just worry if she told him the truth. "I would have come out in a minute, you know," she said softly. "I'm really fine, and you didn't come into the building with me yesterday."

Finally his smile reached his eyes, if only for a second. "This time's different."

"Any reason?"

"Maybe I was doing things wrong up until now."

Instantly the memory of how he'd kissed her a few hours ago rose up in her thoughts. Forbidden, enticing, it warmed her.

"You were doing everything right," she whispered.

A muscle jerked in his cheek. "It's time to go," he repeated gently.

So she quickly bundled Meggie into her carrier and gathered her things. Mick took the diaper bag from her and left her the baby. He took possession of her arm, drawing her to his side.

She understood why when they reached the door of the clinic.

A crowd of reporters was gathered there. Laura didn't see Blossom in their midst. The *Tattle Today TV* reporter had obviously gotten first dibs on the story and now only the slower vultures remained.

As the eager crew attempted to get close to her and

put their microphones and cameras in her face, Mick turned cold, blue-steel eyes on them.

"The lady has a baby. A very young baby," he said. "Have some decency. Think of your own children."

A few looked sheepish and guilty, as if they really did have children they'd just remembered. Others continued to try to crowd in, but the microphones and cameras retreated just a step. There was enough room for Mick to hustle Laura to the truck.

"From now on, you don't leave your house without me," he said once Laura and the baby were safely ensconced in his truck.

For a moment, Laura wanted to protest. She had to be able to survive on her own. Mick wouldn't be here to protect her forever, but then Meggie began to blow bubbles, and Laura remembered that this was a special situation. Hopefully, the police would find the culprit causing all the problems soon. Hopefully that would happen before Mick left. For now, she would be grateful for his protection of her baby. For Meggie, she would accept assistance she normally wouldn't take.

"You didn't think you'd be walking into such a mess when you decided to take this job, did you?" she asked.

He looked at her as he turned the key in the ignition. "Laura, everything about this trip has been a surprise."

"Thank you," she said, impulsively reaching out to cup his jaw with her hand. "For helping us so much."

For two seconds he froze. His skin lay warm and rough beneath her fingers. He swallowed and she felt the movement through her entire body.

"Don't do that," he said softly, fiercely. "Don't touch me. You know where it leads."

Slowly she pulled her fingers away, her skin sliding against his, making her palm itch.

"Thank you," she repeated again, and this time she was thanking him for being the one to remind her she'd done something foolish and risky.

"Hell," he said, then he glanced at Meggie. "I mean 'heck.' Let's get you home. Let's go do something about that bed."

Laura blinked hard, her eyes widened. Then she realized what he was talking about and she chuckled.

It was enough to break the tension. Almost.

"Damn, Laura," Mick said. "I just keep making mistakes with you, don't I?"

Maybe so, Laura thought, but they were such achingly sweet mistakes. Such tender, tempting mistakes.

"Couldn't you just make me a chair?" she asked, thinking she would explode if they spent any more time talking of beds.

Mick studied the situation, then shook his head.

"No, we've got to get you a decent bed and something that resembles a real mattress. You can't do anything with the one you've got."

And this time he didn't apologize for his words. After all, he was right. She'd spent an absolutely sleepless night last night. The reasons were clear, and they were all tied up with Mick and that bed.

She needed a better bed. And Mick, but she'd settle for the bed.

Well, at least he was on the outside of Laura's apartment and she was on the inside, Mick reasoned as he stroked the plane over the piece of wood he'd cut. He'd found a corner of the yard between the house and the garage where Laura's place was located. He'd bargained with the landlord and offered to make him a new glider if he'd let him use this space.

Now Laura was inside making supper, and everything was fine, except he was all too conscious that he was making a bed for a woman he wanted, a bed she might share with another man, but not with him.

"Damn," he said a little too loudly as he nicked his thumb.

As if she'd been listening for the sound of his voice, the window came open and Laura stuck her head out. "What happened? Is something wrong? Did you hurt yourself?"

"It's nothing," he said. "Goes with the territory. I do this all the time."

"Not when you're helping me out," she said. "I'll be right down."

Automatically he reached for the flannel shirt that he'd shed in the unusually warm fall air. His mother had been very clear about how a man should treat a lady, and he'd listened well.

He was just shrugging his shoulders into the shirt when Laura came through the door. For a second she gazed at his bare chest and she stopped. Then, taking a deep breath, she forged onward.

"Let me see," she directed. "Are you bleeding?"

"Did anyone ever tell you that you're beautiful when you're bossy?" he asked her.

She raised her brows at him. "You're not going to

distract me with compliments or questions. Now, give me your hand. I know what I'm doing. I have brothers. Remember?''

He remembered. And she did, indeed, know what she was doing, he thought as she took his big hand in her smaller one. Her skin was soft, her touch was gentle. He wondered why he hadn't thought of cutting himself before if it meant getting this kind of heady attention and the chance to be close enough to breathe in the sweet woman scent of her, to feel the silk of her skin against his.

Of course he shouldn't *be* this close to her.

He started to pull his hand back.

''I promise I'm not going to hurt you,'' she said soothingly, and he almost wanted to groan. She thought he was afraid of her. Well, wasn't he, or at least wasn't he afraid of what she made him feel?

''It's just a scratch,'' he said sternly.

''Scratches get infected.'' She pulled out her small first aid kit and carefully, with soft, nimble fingers, cleaned his wound, then swiftly bandaged it.

''There,'' she said. ''That's better.''

Was it? He'd been pretty much minding his business, making this bed a few minutes ago. Now all he could think of was tugging her close into his arms, up against his chest, leaning forward and taking her lips with his own.

''Thanks,'' he said instead, but at that moment he heard a sound. Small, muffled, a rustle, a slight thud. This house was on the outskirts of town, not close to any other buildings. Foot traffic would be unlikely, and automatically he swiveled to the side, looking out into the darkness where the sound had come from.

"Mick?" Laura moved closer. "What is it?"

He held out one hand to silence her. He listened to the nothingness of the air and the night. He watched the long line of bushes that separated the main house from the wooded area next to it.

Nothing. No sound. No movement.

Still, he waited. He'd heard something.

Then a twig cracked in the distance.

He strode forward. He stared into the gathering gloom, looked for some clue as to which way he should go.

Nothing. No indication. No help. And the silence was growing. Whoever or whatever had been there was gone.

Mick took a deep breath and shook his head.

"It was probably a stray dog," Laura whispered, coming up behind him, her voice strained and cautious. "Or maybe a rabbit."

He turned to see the way she was gazing earnestly out into the darkness.

"Or maybe it could be—"

"Who?"

She looked him directly in the eyes and he saw that hers were troubled. "My sister is still out there. Maybe she thought she could show up here and I'd help her."

"You think so?"

"Not really. This town is probably the last place she wants to be right now. It was no doubt just an animal."

But by now he'd taken down the utility light he'd

been working by. He swung it in a wide arc and moved forward, looking for animal tracks.

Suddenly he stopped. He shone the light on a bit of bare ground next to the bushes. The toeprint of a shoe showed there. Half the person's foot had obviously been in the grass and just the front couple of inches had touched the soft earth. Nothing to go on, Mick thought, except that whoever had been here had not been an animal.

With so little of the print, there was no telling. It could have just been a curious kid or a nosy neighbor who'd heard the sawing and wanted to see what was happening over here. It could have been Clyde, who'd found out that Mick was here snooping around and was wondering what was going on. It could have been Laura's sister, or someone who'd seen that story last night, who liked the Maitlands and who wished Laura ill.

Could have been anyone. An innocent or an enemy. With all the things that had been happening at the clinic, who was to say that the vandals might not move out into the general population...or stalk a Maitland?

Mick looked down at Laura standing there, so slender, so vulnerable and small. Suddenly, he wanted to swear, to wrap her in a bulletproof bodysuit and put her in a protective box to keep her safe.

Instead he took her by the shoulders and looked down into her eyes.

"From now on, when I'm out here working, you stay inside out of sight. All right?"

For a moment he thought she was going to protest, but then the crying of the baby sounded through the open window. She turned to go to her child.

Mick reached for her arm. "Promise me you won't wander out into the night while I'm working. All right, Laura?"

"I won't leave my child alone again," she said softly, then pulled free to go take care of Meggie. "I won't leave her vulnerable."

But who would keep Laura from being vulnerable?

Mick looked around as if looking for the Let's Protect Laura Maitland committee. But, of course, there was no one there.

"Looks like you're elected, buddy," he said to himself. "Stay close to her and that sweet little baby."

There was no question that he would stay as close to the lady as skin.

Except tonight. Tonight he had something to do.

An hour later, Mick sat in his truck at the end of the clinic's drive. He'd trailed Clyde from his hotel to the clinic and watched as Clyde had gone inside half an hour ago. Megan Maitland's car was still in the lot, too. For the hundredth time, Mick wondered what had brought his stepfather back to the town where he couldn't possibly be welcome.

He was starting to slide lower into his seat when the sound of voices brought him upright. Thank goodness the sun had set several hours ago. The red of his truck would be obscured.

Glancing toward the doorway of the clinic, he could catch only snatches of conversation at first. That pleading voice of Clyde's. Something about Connor and Chase.

Connor was Megan's son...and Clyde's. The unborn child that Clyde had deserted. And Chase was

Connor's son. The Maitland ties were tangled. Laura fit in there somewhere, but he couldn't afford to think about her now. He needed to concentrate.

The small group moved closer, almost too close. In the shadows, Hugh Blake became visible. His deep voice cut the night. "Absolutely not. She agreed to meet you here tonight in spite of who you are. You've been hanging around for weeks now, and she's been patient, but tonight you've asked for too much."

Megan's small body seemed to sag against Hugh, and Clyde's voice turned gentle as he soothed and apologized. Mick knew that voice. It meant Clyde was intent on getting his way and would do whatever he had to in order to get it. He'd used that voice on Mick's mother many times. It had never failed to work. Clyde was a master at oozing sincerity. The trick was to figure out when that sincerity was genuine and when it was feigned.

"I'll wait," Clyde said to Megan. "Think about it. I'll abide by your decision when you make it."

His slow, soothing tone seemed to hold conviction. Megan stood up straighter and nodded. She brushed her hand over his sleeve, then took Hugh's arm.

As Clyde moved off to his car, and Megan and Hugh also moved away, Mick wondered what that was all about. He was pretty sure that no one would be talking about this conversation on *Tattle Today TV.* He wondered if anyone but Clyde actually knew what the man's intentions really were. He wondered if they were good and hoped they were.

The man was just too good with secrets. And planning.

Clyde was obviously also good at waiting since he'd been here for weeks, Mick thought with disgust. And now there would be more waiting, more time in Austin. And while he waited for his stepfather to do whatever he'd come here to do, there would be more opportunities to invade Laura's space and her life and possibly hurt her with his driving need of her. Worse, there would be more opportunities to repeat history. Clyde Mitchum's stepson betraying a Maitland woman. Mick's gut wrenched at the thought. He wanted out.

But what was there to do but wait? Clyde had a plan. That was what he'd indicated to him when they'd talked just before Mick had come here. His stepfather's words had filled him with a sense of unease. It was why he'd come here. Clyde was his stepfather, after all, and he was mostly bad, but sometimes good. Besides, Maeve had loved him. She'd wanted him to be so much more than he had been most of the time. She'd counted on Mick to keep his stepdad out of trouble, before and after death. If Clyde was up to something sneaky or dishonorable, Mick wanted to figure out what was going on and stop it. And if Clyde's intentions were honorable? Well, then the man should have a chance to become the man he should have been years ago in this very town. And maybe soon everyone could end the play happy.

But he thought of Laura and hunger filled him.

He couldn't wait much longer for Clyde to show his hand.

Chapter Seven

She'd been wrong to come to Austin.

The thought kept running through Laura's head the next morning as she stared at the beginnings of the headboard for the bed Mick was making. He'd brought it inside and leaned it against the wall. Now she couldn't help running her fingertips over the curving bit of maple.

"There's too much going on with the Maitlands, isn't there, Meggie?" she whispered to her baby, who was staring at the angel mobile high above the white crib where she lay. "We're starting to owe too many people. Look at this crib Megan loaned us. And Mick. What was I thinking to let him start doing this many things for me? You and I have to be careful, sweetness. We've seen what happens to women who rely too much on others. They start needing people and wanting things they can't have."

Meggie blinked big silent eyes at her mother, and Laura scooped up her child and cuddled her close.

"Just you and me, sweetie. Just you and me. We can't get too attached to him. He's not ours for real, you know."

But she felt her throat growing tight, her eyes growing hot, and so she shook herself and blinked hard.

"Big talk, huh, when the man will be here to pick us up and take us to work in just a few minutes? Still, we've got to pull back. We're starting to worry him. That something he thought he saw yesterday. Probably nothing. We shouldn't worry him. We'll just be careful and start edging away. Maybe I'll borrow one of Rafe's cars. How about that? Would you like to ride with Mom?"

But Meggie only kicked her feet...until Mick showed up.

"Hi, darlin'," he said in that achingly mesmerizing tone made to get a woman's attention. Any woman's attention, young or old, apparently, because with those two simple words, Laura noted that her daughter grew alert. She cooed and tracked Mick's movements.

Not good. Definitely time to bow out, Laura told herself. After all, she didn't really need someone to drive her around or make her furniture or protect her and Meggie.

But staring into Mick's let-me-make-love-to-you-darlin' blue eyes, she wanted him. Desperately. She was just as bad as Meggie, but at least she had the benefit of experience. She could do something about her weaknesses.

* * *

"You're quiet today," Mick said as he helped Laura gather Meggie's diaper bag and some books Laura was taking to the center to read to the younger children. "You're worrying. I promise I won't let anyone hurt you or Meggie. No one will get near you."

The deep break in his voice made her heart ache to touch him, to assure him that her worries had nothing to do with any physical danger she and Meggie might be in. There was, after all, no one who would have any real reason to be following her around. And she certainly couldn't tell him she was worried that she was starting to feel too much for him. After all, wasn't he a man who'd made it clear he was just here to do a job? He wasn't one for relationships. If she told him the truth, he'd only be angry at himself.

"I'm not afraid, Mick," she said softly. "We'll be fine. Actually, I was thinking about borrowing a car from Rafe. I really should start getting used to the streets of Austin, get back into this driving thing."

"Not yet," he said, his eyes dark and serious.

"You'll be leaving soon, though, won't you? Isn't the job moving along more quickly than you'd anticipated? I thought I heard someone say that at the clinic. Your reason for being here won't even exist much longer."

He blinked. Just the slightest movement. The directness of his gaze looked suddenly less direct before it settled into the warmth she was used to seeing.

"I don't have to leave just yet," he said simply.

"You don't have any family that will be missing you? I never asked that, did I?"

"No one who'll be missing me." But she noted that

he hadn't said that he didn't have family. Suddenly Laura felt sick.

"Mick?"

"Don't look like that, sunshine," he said. "What's wrong?"

"It just occurred to me, you're not—you're not married, are you? I mean, you did say that you weren't the marrying kind, but men...say things sometimes that don't always mean what they seem to mean."

And suddenly he was close to her, reaching for her. "I'm not the marrying kind," he said angrily. "Never have been. Never will be. I don't have a wife, so you don't have to start worrying that in being here with me, you've been betraying another woman. There's no woman."

But there was something. She could see it in his eyes. He wasn't telling her everything. Well, what had she expected? This was the way it was. Some things never changed where Maitland women like her mother and herself were concerned.

"I'd better get to work," she said. "I'm sorry for what I said."

And he placed his hand on her arm. "Don't. You had a right to ask. You've got a baby to think of."

A baby that was starting to squeal. Automatically, Mick leaned down to where she lay in her carrier.

"Shh, little one," he crooned. "You're safe. Nothing to cry over."

At the sound of his voice, her squealing stopped mid-note. Mick ducked his head, his look stunned and...entranced.

Laura couldn't help chuckling. "She recognizes the way you sound, and she likes it."

Mick put out one finger and stroked the baby's cheek. "So small and fragile," he said, and he said it as if he were afraid of that fragility.

"She's stronger than you think. You could pick her up," she said again, seeing that he wanted to but was wary.

Instantly he rose. "I'll carry your things," he told her, taking the diaper bag and the books.

When they got to the clinic a short time later, Blossom Woodward was waiting for them.

"Ms. Maitland, I'd like to speak with you," she said, crowding in close.

Mick stepped between her and Laura. "The lady has things to do."

"I'm aware of where she's going, Mr. Hannon, but I just have a question."

"It seems you've asked a lot of questions about Laura already. You've planted suspicions in people's minds. She had to move out of the boardinghouse where she was staying."

For just a trace of a second, something almost akin to guilt strayed into Blossom's eyes. Then she shook her head. "I just want to know about Luke, Ms. Maitland," she said.

Up until this time, Laura had been merely trying to get between Blossom and Mick. She just couldn't have the man fighting her battles for her. Now, however, a deep current of anger zipped through her.

"Leave Luke out of this, please," she said, raising her chin in a challenge. Her older brother had borne the brunt of so much when he was growing up. He had felt responsible for his mother's unhappiness and had tried to protect her and his siblings. "You don't need him."

But the mere fact that she had responded to Blossom's questions seemed to feed the lady's need to know. She surged forward and Laura had to turn her back on the woman.

Mick stayed with her all the way to the day-care center. They had barely entered the room when the sound of Megan's voice drifted down the hallway.

"This is something I don't feel comfortable with, Clyde."

"I know I said I'd wait, but he's my son, Megan. You and I made him. I've changed over the years."

"I—I'd like to believe that."

"Believe it. Give me a chance." His voice sounded whiny, manipulative, pleading.

"I—I can't talk about this right now," Megan said.

And she shouldn't be listening, Laura thought. This conversation was taking place out in the hallway, and Megan sounded distressed, as if she wasn't even aware that she was holding a private discussion in a public place.

Laura moved to put some distance between herself and the doorway so that she couldn't hear. She turned to thank Mick for taking her part against Blossom.

He had frozen in his tracks, backed up against the interior wall. He looked down at her and shook his head, reaching out to stroke one long finger down her cheek.

"Don't ever let a man manipulate you, Laura," he

said, indicating that he, too, had heard Megan's conversation. "Not again. You're too good for that. You deserve a better kind of man. The very best life has to offer."

For two seconds she froze, feeling the echo of his touch against her skin. He smiled suddenly, gently, then backed away and opened the door leading to the emergency exit of the day-care center.

"Later," he said gently.

But she knew there wouldn't be many more "laters." Soon his job would be done, her bed would be done, and only the echo of his voice in her head would remind her and Meggie of the man.

And the memory of his touch. She placed one hand against her cheek and held it there.

She wondered what it would be like if she and Mick ever both let their defenses down and gave in to the heat that flickered to life every time they came too close.

Don't, she thought. Touching Mick that way would be incredibly dangerous and risky.

But she was her own woman. Couldn't she take a risk or two if she wanted to?

In the end, the kind of risk she elected to take was very different from the one she had been thinking of. When Mick showed up the next day to pick her up for work, she was running a bit late and she was slightly flustered because of it, but not too flustered to realize that the man was looking more than a little tired.

"You were up too late last night, weren't you?"

she asked, gazing up into his blue eyes. He'd been pushing himself, trying to finish as much of the bed as he could so that she wouldn't have to keep sleeping on the one in the apartment that had a tendency to come apart at the joints, letting the mattress slip down onto the floor at one corner. Let's face it, she thought, he's just been spending altogether too much time on me.

He smiled a tired smile. "I'm perfectly fine, darlin'. Don't get that look on your face."

"What look?"

"Your nurse's look. You told me that you've studied nursing. I'm lucky to be getting such expert care," he said, holding up his finger with the bandage on it. She'd changed it again yesterday. "And I'm grateful, but you're not going to start fussing over me. You've got too many things to worry about as it is. Besides, I was only here until ten o'clock last night."

It had been past ten, but she wouldn't call him on that. She raised her brows. "Yes, but you'd put in a full day of work before that."

Of course, he hadn't put in quite a full day of work, because every day he was here, picking her up to drive her. She still hadn't called Rafe about the car.

Finally, a thought occurred to her. Maybe Mick wasn't tired from staying too late at her house. Maybe he was worried. His boss, for all he joked about the man, might be giving him grief for the time he took off to give her a ride. It would be just like Mick to insist there was no problem when there really was. He did things like that, kept them inside, tried to keep people from worrying. He protected people.

It was a reminder once again that he was a man with secrets, a man who had dark stories hiding behind that blue-eyed smile of his, a man who wasn't ever going to completely open up to her. A small trickle of pain slipped through her, but it was quickly replaced by guilt. The secrets she couldn't do anything about. It was just the way some men were. She knew that better than anyone, and it wasn't going to affect her, not if she didn't allow herself to feel too much for Mick.

But the business of letting him take grief from his boss over taking care of her, well, that was completely her fault and her responsibility. She would take care of that today.

"Laura?"

She looked up at Mick and realized that he had been staring down at her, maybe for some time. A blush warmed her skin.

"I guess I zoned out," she said.

"You're feeling all right?"

She was feeling great. For once, she was going to get to help Mick instead of letting him help her. And she knew right when she was going to do it, too.

"Excuse me, but could you tell me who Mick Hannon's supervisor is?" Laura asked the burly man reading the newspaper. It was early the next morning, too early for Mick to have arrived yet. She had begged Rafe for a temporary loaner of one of his cars, and he had been thrilled that she was finally letting him do something for her. Now she just hoped that Mick's boss was already here.

"You want Mick's boss?" the burly man asked, as if she'd just asked to speak to the president of the United States.

"I—yes, I do. Is that a problem?"

"Mick in trouble?"

She smiled at the concern in the man's voice, glad to see that Mick's co-workers worried about him.

"No, I just have a question to ask the man. Do you know who his boss is? Who could I talk to who would be responsible for him?"

The man scratched his head. He looked to the side where another man was just showing up. Laura refrained from glancing at her watch. She'd been lucky to get here before Mick did. She'd only done that by gambling that his supervisor would need to be there before his crew, but if she didn't hurry, Mick would arrive and she didn't want him to know she was here.

"Excuse me, sir?" she prompted.

He shook his head. "Well, I suppose you could talk to Dell, but he's not here. Ned's the project supervisor, the guy over there, with the glasses. Mick's not in some kind of trouble with the Maitlands, is he?"

"Mick? Never," she assured him, "and thank you for the information."

She hurried over to the man with the glasses. He looked up from his paper and studied her.

"Good morning, Mr.—"

"Romney," he said. "Can I help you?"

Nervousness descended. Mick wouldn't like her being here. His boss might not, either. But—

"I'm Laura Maitland, Mr. Romney," she said, wading in, "and I wanted to speak to you about Mick

Hannon. It's occurred to me that he may be having trouble here at work, and I wanted to let you know that he's been trying to help me. He's a very kind man, and I've been a bit of a burden on him lately. You probably heard about him helping with the birth of my baby and in other ways. I want you to know that we're on our feet again. So, I hope you'll take that into consideration when you're reviewing his work performance. He's—such a good man.''

The man's eyes had grown wide behind his glasses. He picked up a cup of coffee and took a big swig. ''You're here because you're worried that I might chew Mick out about missing time on the job?''

He sounded as if she'd just asked him to sleep with her, as if that was the last thing he'd ever expected her to say.

''I just wanted to assure you that he can keep more regular hours from here on out.'' Her voice felt a bit smaller. She wondered if it really sounded that way.

Suddenly the man smiled kindly. ''I think you're a little mistaken, Ms. Maitland. I'm not Mick's boss.''

She blinked. ''But you're the project manager. That's what someone said.''

He laughed at that. ''That's me, all right, and that's what I do, but—'' He held out his hands palm up. ''Dell's the big boss up in Dallas, but here, well, most of the time the rest of us answer to Mick.''

If her skin had felt warm before, now it felt red hot. ''I see. Thank you.'' She started to turn away, then changed her mind. ''So you mean there's no need for me to worry about Mick losing his job?''

He grinned. ''We'd be a lot more lost without him

than the other way around. No need to worry, Ms. Maitland.''

Maybe not, she thought as she picked up Meggie at the center and went back to her car. She didn't have to worry about Mick getting fired, but she still didn't know much about him.

Mick hadn't actually lied to her about his job, because she'd never really asked what position he held, but the truth was that he'd been a stranger just under two weeks ago, and he was still a stranger in many ways. She'd been there before with a man. It wasn't a good place to go.

''Heard you had a princess trying to save your sorry butt this morning.'' Dell Douglas's booming voice came over the receiver and Mick grimaced. Dell was a good friend, the owner of the construction firm, but his words recalled what he'd learned about Laura this morning. She'd come here on a mission to save him and learned what he probably should already have told her. Except he was trying to keep a low profile, and he didn't have any reason to give her for that. He certainly couldn't tell her that he was here in town to spy on his stepfather.

''She's pretty special, Dell,'' he said.

''Must be, if she likes you. How special is she?''

''Don't go there, Dell.''

''I see.'' And Mick just bet his friend *did* see. Dell always had been way too perceptive about a man's weaknesses. ''Well, how about this, then? You give any more thought to taking over the business when you get back home? I can't live forever, Mick.''

"You'd better," Mick said, and his voice was gruff. Clyde might be his stepfather, but Dell had been a good fill-in over the years. It was a rotten shame that the man had never married and had kids. He would have been a great family man. As it was, he gave a significant amount of his affection to his employees. Mick was his favorite. "Don't even think about retiring, Dell. You're the guts of this place. You make things happen."

The man chuckled. "Nice try, Mick, but I'm going to retire soon, like it or not. I want to travel. I want to rest. And speaking of making things happening, how's that addition going?"

"Right on target. We'll be finishing up the basics in a few weeks. Time for the next wave to come in."

"You'll be finishing up that other, too?"

"The other?"

Dell snorted. "I've known you too long, Mick. I know Clyde's there. I know he's up to something and that you're up to your old tricks, making sure he doesn't do anything too illegal if you can stop him. It's not the job a son or a stepson should have to take on."

"We play the cards we're handed, Dell."

"Yeah, we do, and it looks like you've been handed a chance at a pretty little woman who cares enough to march into a crew of toughened construction workers and plead your case. Think on that, Mick."

"See you in a few weeks, Dell."

And Mick hung up the phone. Now he just had to explain to Laura why he hadn't told her the truth about himself. Somehow. He remembered all the times he'd told her that he had an understanding boss, which was true, but which wasn't as simple as it sounded. He remembered that she'd been deceived by men before.

"Hell," he said beneath his breath. He didn't want to deceive her. He wanted to tell her everything, promise her everything, lay all his cards on the table and ask her to take a chance on him.

Which would be a mistake. It was a chance he wouldn't let her take even if she wanted to.

It was no chance at all.

Still, he had to talk to her. Right away.

Chapter Eight

"I hear you're driving now." Mick stood in the doorway of Laura's apartment in the early afternoon light, looking down into her startled eyes as she let him inside. He tried to tamp down the sense of panic he was feeling, but it wasn't working. He'd seen the blue sedan in the driveway and it wasn't the landlord's. If she didn't need transportation, she didn't need him for much anymore. That should feel good.

It didn't.

Instead, all he could think was that he'd never seen anything more beautiful than the green of her eyes or the sheen of her long brown hair. There was pride in those eyes...and deep determination to stand on her own. He needed to respect that.

She nodded. "I was just going to call and let you know I wouldn't need a ride. Rafe is taking Greer out of town for two days for a lovers' getaway, but he was more than happy to lend me one of his toys before he left. We didn't have a car when I was small. He's like a kid with them now.''

He smiled. "I understand.''

She took a deep breath. "It's hard to understand poverty if you've never been there.''

"But if you've been there, you do understand.''

Laura looked directly into his eyes then. "Yes, you would,'' she whispered. "The things I'm finding out about you today, Mick Hannon,'' and she smiled slightly, shaking her head.

He cleared his throat and reached out to take her hand. "It takes a pretty brave woman to march into a crowd of heavily muscled men and argue for justice.'' His voice was thick. He just couldn't help it.

She ducked her head, her hair swooping forward. "Yes, well, that was pretty silly of me, wasn't it?''

And any intelligent thoughts he might have been having slid right out the door. He tucked one finger beneath her chin, tilted her head upward and lowered his head to hers.

"It was the nicest thing anyone's done for me,'' he said fiercely, just before his lips claimed hers. And she had the most delicious mouth he'd ever tasted. Slowly he kissed her. Again. And yet again. He wanted to keep her there against him for hours, but he finally pulled away. Her hands rested on his chest.

"Nice or not, it was silly of me, Mick. You're the boss.'' Her voice was a strained whisper.

"But you didn't know I was the boss. I never told you.''

"I know. I just assumed.''

And maybe he shouldn't have let her assume. He

shouldn't have said all those things about having an understanding boss, but hell, it wasn't the kind of thing a man went around announcing. It felt too much like swaggering. It felt like…Clyde, who had always loved to talk himself up.

"You worried about me," he said softly, tracing a line from her earlobe down her jaw, then kissing the tip of her chin. "Don't worry about me, Laura. I don't want you to have to worry about anything, but I'm incredibly touched that you did. I'm grateful."

And he slid his hands up behind her back and brought her in close so that he could taste her all over again.

She rose on her toes and met him kiss for kiss. Her lips were like soft pink candy, the inside of her mouth sweeter still. Feeling her skin beneath his hands was like dropping a match on a pile of dry paper. Desire flared out of control, and he wanted to feel more of her, as much as he could have.

Slipping his palms up her sides, over her breasts, he rested them there, letting their warmth sink in, reveling as her nipples hardened beneath the pads of his thumbs. Having her this warm and close was enough to make a man never want to use his hands for touching anything but her ever again.

Laura moaned softly. "Mick?" She pressed against him, then twisted so that she filled his palms. She wrapped her arms around his neck and kissed him with fervor and eagerness.

For five seconds he had her. Her body was his. He was on his way to heaven. He was going to have all of her.

Tearing his lips from hers, he looked around…and found there was no bed that would take his weight, no couch that was long enough to make love on. Only the hardness of the floor.

He thought of her soft skin against the rough floor. He thought of how careless another man had been of her, and he ripped himself away from her. Immediately, before he could do something he'd hate himself for, ever after. Drinking in big gulps of air, he did his best to get his desire for her under control. He took a step back, hoping that would make it easier. It didn't.

"Laura, angel, I'm so sorry."

She looked up at him. "Why? Because you wanted me? Because I wanted you so badly I lost sight of everything else? That's not your fault. After all, you're a—"

He was pretty darn sure she'd been planning to say that he was a man. It was what she knew of men for the most part, that they took what they wanted, even when they weren't meaning to stay, as they both knew he wasn't. And wasn't that just what he'd been intending to do?

"You were just giving in to the moment," she said softly. "So was I, but—"

"Don't put more blame on yourself than on me," he warned. "We both know this isn't a good idea, even if it's a terribly seductive idea. It's a damn hard thing to fight off when every time I look at you, I want to be inside you. I want you any way I can have you as long as your skin is touching mine. Laura, I want you so badly I can barely remember to breathe in air, but—" He shook his head. "A man who can't control himself when the situation demands it isn't much of a man.''

She smiled up at him then, tremulously, gently. She actually dared the fates and reached out to stroke his cheek. ''You're very much of a man, Mick,'' she said softly. ''And I want you like that, too. I guess we'll just have to fight it.''

He *was* fighting it, every hour of every day, but he nodded because she needed reassurance. She needed to be safe, and dammit, he *wanted* her to feel safe. From him and from anyone else who threatened her.

''Are you...are you happy in Austin, Laura?'' he asked suddenly. ''There haven't been any more reporters I don't know about bothering you?''

''I'm doing okay,'' she agreed. ''The children at the day-care center are turning out to be little angels, Meggie loves it there, and Megan and her family have all been wonderful to me. Things seem to be settling down a bit. Janelle's still out there, but there's no sign of her around here. They haven't figured out what happened with those security cameras, but nothing else has happened at the clinic since then. Maybe that will be the end of it. I just wish I knew where Luke was. Rafe and I haven't had any luck in locating him, and that reporter is still looking for him, I think. She asked Megan about him.''

''You're worried about him.''

She shrugged. ''I know he's older than I am, but he's my brother. How could I not worry?''

He smiled. ''Not having a brother, I can't answer that, but I'm sure you're right.''

''No sisters, either?''

Her voice was so sad that he couldn't help brushing a lock of hair back from her face, just to connect with her in some small way.

"I had a mother, Laura. She loved me."

"Mine loved me, too, which was good since my father was never around. Did you have a father?"

"Not much of one. I had a stepfather." But he wasn't going to talk about that. That would only lead to questions he couldn't answer right now.

"I'd better get to work," he said, stepping back. "I don't want to leave you with only half a bed."

Laura took a deep breath. She stepped back, too. "Of course. You're running out of time."

"We still have some," he said, correcting her. And he had darn well better use it right.

She'd certainly struck a chord by mentioning Mick's father, hadn't she? Laura thought the next day as she helped a four-year-old darling into some dress-up clothes at the center. She could almost see him shutting down, closing himself off when she had led the conversation in that direction. No question about it, he was definitely a man with walls and secrets.

A man who worried about her and tempted her and called her baby "sweetheart" even if he wouldn't touch her.

A man she had no business spending so much time thinking about, she reminded herself, and went off to settle a minor dispute involving two children and one teddy bear.

"You're very good at that, you know." A soft female voice sounded behind her and Laura whirled to find Megan watching her. "You're a natural mother. It's a gift."

"Thank you." Laura couldn't help smiling. "If it's a gift, then it's one you seem to possess in abundance. I've seen you with the nurses and the other employees here. They all love you and look up to you. They trust you for…everything."

She couldn't help the slight catch in her voice. She'd loved her mother, but trust hadn't ever really been a part of that equation, not when her mother would sacrifice everything, including her dignity and her children's sense of security to try to be with the man she'd loved and couldn't have.

"Trust is important," she added, and then realized that Megan hadn't responded to her previous comment. In fact, the older woman was looking somewhat distressed.

"Megan, are you all right? Come on, let's get you a place to sit."

Amazingly enough, Megan, the heart of the clinic, nodded. She followed Laura to a small room where the employees of the center took their coffee breaks. It had a small refrigerator and a couch. "Can I get you something to drink?" Laura asked.

Megan shook her head, looking a bit lost, then she took a deep breath. "I'm fine. Really. I'm sorry for letting my mind wander so. There've just been a few things on my mind lately, things I have difficulty talking about. I don't want to tell my children, either. My troubles would only worry them."

"It's difficult keeping everything inside yourself," Laura agreed. She'd frequently hidden her feelings as a child. Actually, she'd hidden them as an adult, too, and still did.

"Your comment about trust just…set me off," Megan admitted. "It's an issue I'm struggling with myself. A lot lately. I have the feeling you know something about trust."

"I'm a bit of an expert," Laura admitted. "Lots of practice dealing with the untrustworthy."

Megan studied that comment for a moment. "Would you—that is, I'm sure you know something of my situation, my past. Everyone around here does. The Maitlands have no secrets. What would you do if the man who'd once betrayed you came back and asked you to trust him, to give him a chance to prove that he had become a worthy man?"

For a moment a vision of Greg's face flashed in Laura's mind. She was surprised to realize that she didn't feel particularly distressed at the vision.

"You're talking about Mr. Mitchum?"

"Yes, Mr. Mitchum. Clyde wants to meet his son. He's been pressing me lately. After all these years, he wants to see Connor, and Chase as well. He tells me that he's a different man, and maybe he is. Time does make a difference in lives. We change even if we don't want to change. Maybe he's got good intentions. If that's so, would I be robbing him and my son and grandson if I didn't allow them to meet? And if I did allow them to meet, and Clyde hurt my child and my grandchild, what then?"

"Then you would help them by showing them that you love them just as much as ever. They'd still have you."

Megan nodded. "They'll always have me. So you think I should give Clyde a chance?"

Laura dropped onto the couch where Megan was already seated.

"I'd like to help you, Megan, but I can't help you make this decision. It's too personal. The questions are too big."

"The question is enormous," Megan agreed, patting Laura's arm. "Once a man has lost a woman's trust, once he's wounded her deeply, can she ever really and truly trust that man again?"

It was, Laura admitted to herself later that night as she said a prayer for Megan, a question no woman ever wanted to have to answer. She hoped she'd never face a situation such as that.

Mick stared down into Laura's worried eyes that evening.

"Clyde Mitchum wants her to let him meet his son and his grandson," she said slowly. "She doesn't know whether she can trust him. I didn't know what to tell her. I couldn't begin to put myself in her shoes. If a man betrayed a woman and then came back and wanted to change, how would that woman feel? How could she ever truly trust him again? I could see that she wanted to think it was possible that he was a new man, but I don't know if it is truly possible. Or at least, even if it is possible, I don't know if I could be forgiving. What do you do about a man like that?"

Mick's throat felt tight, as if words couldn't escape their constricting bonds. He swallowed hard.

"I hope you never have to find out."

And then she smiled. A little. "Oh, I don't think you have to worry about Greg ever having a change of heart. He made it pretty clear that my child and I were not socially significant enough trash as far as he was concerned. My mother's history as a Vegas showgirl was something he couldn't get past. He won't be bothering us."

But it wasn't Greg that he'd been thinking of. More than ever, he wanted to go down on his knees and tell her everything, but to what purpose? To ease his conscience? That wouldn't fly. Clyde might have been a man, but he had always acted like a child. Mick was responsible for him. And if he was finally standing up and trying to act like the man he should always have been, shouldn't he have the chance to do that without intervention from anyone? Mick would not stand behind him like some stern, disapproving parent demanding that his son do the right thing. If he came forward, all of Clyde's good intentions would be spoiled. And what if Clyde's intentions weren't good at all?

Then he needed to be found out and stopped, hopefully before he'd done too much damage.

"Mick?" Laura was looking at him with worried eyes.

He stroked one finger down her cheek. "If your Greg did come back, Rafe and I would send him packing, angel. No one is going to hurt you."

He was not going to hurt her, because he was just going to take care of his business and get out of here, before deep emotions were involved. With a little luck, there would be no problem.

Hours later, Mick wasn't so sure. He'd tracked Clyde down and found him leaving the hospital, an immensely satisfied look on his face.

Behind him, Hugh Blake stood, his expression thunderous.

The situation, whatever it might be, was clearly escalating. He couldn't help wondering what this meant, for himself and for the Maitlands.

But there was only one Maitland in his mind. One who mattered most.

There was tension in the air the next day at the clinic, and even more tension when he arrived at Laura's house to work on her nearly completed bed frame.

"I heard that Megan is going to arrange for Clyde to meet with his son," he said, figuring that the smartest thing was to wade right in and get past the day's news.

Laura nodded. "Yes, everyone was a bit fidgety today. We're all hoping that this is a good thing for Megan. She's had so many bad things happen to her."

She wasn't the only woman who'd faced pain, though, Mick reasoned. His mother had. Laura had.

But Laura's past wasn't really his business. He was here just to finish this bed, deal with Clyde and get out of town.

The bed needed only a coat or two of linseed oil to finish it, and then a mattress to round things out. Then his beauty could get her sleep and the world could go to hell for all he cared.

But it didn't look like anyone was going to get any

sleep tonight. He had barely finished rubbing in the oil when he came inside to the sound of Meggie crying.

Her tiny baby sobs turned into wails. Her little face was red and cross. His heart went out to her, and to Laura who was clearly scared.

"I called her pediatrician," she said. "He said it sounded like a tummy ache. But she's so miserable. I—"

"Shh, angel. I know you didn't do anything wrong, so don't go blaming yourself. I'm sure the doctor told you the same thing."

From the look on her face, he could tell that he was right—and that she wasn't completely buying into that whole scenario.

"What do we do?" he asked softly, and his words seemed to calm Laura, balance her. She squared her shoulders.

"We walk her, we rock her, we rub her tummy. We just try to make her comfortable until it goes away and she can sleep."

She walked as she spoke to him. One hand rubbed over the baby's tiny back, one supported her little body.

Meggie sobbed as if her heart would break, and Laura looked so worn and tired and scared. A thought occurred to him.

"Have you been carrying her around and walking her all the time that I've been outside working?"

"There was nothing you could do to help," she said, "so don't go getting all noble and bossy on me."

She thought there had been nothing he could do to

help, because up until this point he hadn't picked up the baby. Not once, he acknowledged. Because he was afraid of what he'd feel if he held that tiny body, because he didn't want to grow close to Meggie any more than he wanted to grow close to Laura. He didn't want this precious little girl to get to know him when he would turn his back on her and walk away soon.

But she was hurting, and Laura was hurting, too. Maybe even more. Psychological hurts could be worse than physical pain, and she was definitely worried to death about her baby. Her arms had to be heavy even if the baby was light.

"I'll—I'll carry her for a while," he managed to say, his voice rough and thick and half uncertain.

Laura stopped dead in her tracks. "You don't have to do that," she whispered.

He knew then that he wanted to. He'd brought her into the world. If she was in pain, he wanted to help.

Wordlessly, he reached out. He took the feather-weight, baby-powder-scented little body in his arms. She was so small, his hands felt too big and rough, but he didn't let go. He walked, he rubbed her little back, and after a while, he began to hum a little song.

"Hush little baby," Laura whispered with a tiny smile. "Soft words for such a big man."

He hoped he wasn't growing red. "My mother used to sing it to me," he said gruffly.

"Mine, too," she answered quietly. And together they walked, they hummed, they sang. They passed Meggie back and forth through the hours.

Finally, the baby slept. As Mick lowered her gently into the crib, she looked like a little angel. He said so, and Laura smiled. She moved the broken ceramic angel that her mother had cherished and placed it on a window ledge within view of Meggie's bed. "Maybe her grandma can't see her, but she can give a gift to her just the same. An angel for the angel," Laura said, with love in her eyes as she watched her child sleep and breathe deep, painless breaths.

Mick couldn't help himself then. He reached out and traced Laura's brow. "She looks so much like you in so many ways," he said. "The arch of your brow. And the tilt of your nose." He lightly touched the bridge of her nose. "And that stubborn, lovely little chin."

He cupped her chin in his palm and lowered his head, just touching his lips to the soft skin of her chin.

She breathed in deeply, almost a gasp, and he raised his head. Her eyes were wide and full of naked desire.

"Easy, angel," he said, touching his lips to hers. And then she was in his arms, filling in the empty spaces. He wanted to hold her there forever. He wondered if his father and his stepfather had ever felt that way about a woman. No doubt they had. No doubt the feeling passed.

To hell with that. For the moment he could kiss her. He could hold her.

And he slid her closer in against his heart. He bent his head and kissed the open vee of her dress. She shuddered against him, and he nearly went mad. Reaching up, he flicked open the first three buttons of her dress. With a twist of his wrist, he unfastened her bra and bared her pale skin to him.

While he watched, her nipple budded before him,

and he thought he'd die if he didn't taste her. He leaned. Lightly he blew on her skin, puckering the nipple tighter. And then he bent lower. He tasted the honey, he sucked the pretty pink bud into his mouth.

She surged into his hand, she twisted against him.

"Mick." Her voice was helpless, needy. "Please. Please, now. It's too much," she said as he withdrew his lips and stroked her lightly with his fingers. "Too much. I want—"

Her words fell away as she began to lose control, as he began to toss all caution out the window. "It's too much," she had said, and the words stuck in his brain. Against his will as he fought it, a vision of what tomorrow would mean to her if he didn't stop slammed into Mick like a rocket going full force.

Roughly, he dragged his body from hers. With shaky fingers, he covered her and undid the damage to her clothing that he'd done.

"I'm so sorry," he said. "I lost my head, angel, and my only excuse is that I've never wanted anything so badly in my life as I wanted you." And still wanted her. Painfully. Madly.

She was struggling to breathe, to compose herself, but she shook her head. "I wanted you, too, but you stopped. You did. Thank you. If we hadn't stopped, I—"

"You would have hated yourself in the morning. Do you think I didn't know that?" It was all that had kept him from sweeping away every barrier that lay between them.

She shook her head harder. "I'm not sure I would have hated myself in the morning. Not at all. I rather think I would have awakened with a big smile on my face, but down the road, there would have been a price to pay."

He swallowed hard. There might have been a very high price for her to pay, and he might have been long gone. He had a bad feeling that she wouldn't have contacted him, no matter what.

"If something had happened, I wouldn't have left you alone to deal with it," he said, but her small smile told him that she thought that such words were too easy to say.

"Thank you," she said. "For saying that and for thinking of my future. Anyway, Dr. Abby won't have cause to reprimand me now. I'm not supposed to be doing this so soon after having a baby, anyway."

And he swore at himself beneath his breath. He should have known. He should have thought.

"It was meant to make you laugh, Mick. Not look like a bear who wanted to maul himself. You did the gentlemanly thing."

But all he could remember was grabbing her, trying to seduce her.

"I should go," he said. "It's late." And his words had them both turning toward the clock. It was four in the morning. In only a little over two hours, dawn would break.

He headed toward the door.

"Mick?"

"Don't beat up on yourself. It was good to be wanted."

He nearly slammed his fist into the wall. He almost

turned around and headed back to tug her into his arms and seal her lips to his once more.

"I've never inspired that kind of passion before," she said, her voice slightly dazed.

And he did turn and look at her then, one brow raised in disbelief. "Your Greg must have been even dumber than I thought at first, angel."

She smiled at him broadly then.

"Yes, he missed out on Meggie, didn't he? You didn't. You were here for her the day she was born and you were here for her tonight, Mick. Don't ever regret tonight, okay?"

A vision of the sleeping baby that he'd helped to soothe rose up before him. "Okay," he agreed. He wouldn't regret that, but he would not be able to forgive himself for the other. Not just because he'd almost had her beneath him on the floor, but because now he couldn't get the image of what it would have been like out of his head.

He fought it off and went home. Two hours later when his alarm went off and he flipped on the television for the morning news update, he found one more reason not to forget the evening before.

Blossom Woodward was on the tube with a special morning report. It seems a very expensive painting was missing from the clinic. Laura and Luke Maitland were her prime suspects.

"I'll be damned if they try to pin this on you, angel," he promised her as he readied himself to head out the door.

He wasn't sure what he was going to do, but he was definitely going to do something.

Chapter Nine

Laura knew who the impatient person at the door was, even before Mick said, "I know it's early, angel, but open the door."

"It's damn early," her brother Rafe said from behind her as she moved to the door. "Too early for a man to be calling on you, Laura. Let me take this and you go change from your bathrobe into something more...you know, something more..."

"Voluminous?" his wife, Greer, asked with a chuckle. "Go on, Laura, get the door. I'll take care of this bear of a brother of yours."

"Laura?" Mick pounded harder, and Laura moved to open the door. She hoped she wasn't blushing, but with Rafe's words she *was* very aware of her half-dressed state.

So deal with it, she told herself. Mick was here early, he'd obviously heard the bad news, he was clearly worried and she didn't intend to let him worry any longer. Rafe's fears about her half-dressed state and Mick's likely reaction were unfounded, anyway. She looked like hell gone bad in the early morning hours.

Still, when she pulled back the door and looked up into Mick's fierce blue eyes, an instant vision of herself half naked and wanton in his arms the night before rolled into place in her mind. She took a deep breath. She stepped back.

"Are you all right?" he asked, his voice a low whisper as he moved forward and waltzed her back into the room, clicking the door shut behind him.

She nodded just as Rafe growled out "She's fine."

Mick glanced at Rafe. "Good morning, Maitland," he said. "Greer." His voice warmed as he looked at Rafe's bemused wife. "Sorry to have interrupted. I was—"

"You were worried about Laura. Like we were," she said, elbowing her husband. "You must have seen Blossom Woodward's spot this morning. Rafe and I had just gotten back from a two-day trip to South Padre when we heard the news and came right over. Laura, fortunately, doesn't have a television set."

Instantly, Mick's eyes grew dark. "Anyone who would imply that Laura would do anything low like that doesn't know the first thing about her."

His voice was deep, warm, filled with conviction. Laura looked up at him and saw that there was no doubt in his eyes. She worried that he'd made her into some sort of angelic person that she would never be and would never want to be.

She opened her mouth, but Rafe was already speaking. "Darn right about that. Laura used to cry when I stepped on ants. She doesn't have a mean drop of blood in her."

And in spite of the frightening news about the clinic's problems and the suspicions that were closing in on her, she felt a moment of gratitude and sadness.

"Thank you for believing in me," she told the three people standing before her, "but I'm not a saint, and there's ample reason to believe I might be involved. It was a very valuable painting, I understand." And she looked around her slightly shabby, obviously inexpensive apartment. She was a woman who could use a bit of financial aid.

"We're not ever going to stand by and let anyone criticize you, sweetie," Greer told her, putting her arms around her new sister-in-law and giving her a quick hug. "Not even you. Rafe's told me all about how you looked after him so patiently when he was growing up. Anyone who could put up with the kind of wild child my husband must have been as a little boy and still love him to pieces has got to be a good woman in my book." Her tone was filled with affection, and her husband groaned and came to her, taking her in his arms.

"She's right, hon. I'm prepared to bust a lot of bones if anyone tries to say one bad thing about you."

"Thanks, squirt," she said, calling him by the nickname she'd planted on him as a child. "I appreciate it and love you for it, but I don't think I'm going to win any points if we leave a trail of broken bodies behind us."

Her words were brave, but her voice cracked

slightly. What if something did happen to her? Meggie would be without a mother.

As if on cue, the baby began to squirm in her crib. Mick looked at Laura and shook his head. He moved to the crib and lifted the baby into his arms, cuddling her close and whispering soothing words to her as she adjusted to the new sensation of being awake.

"Don't worry, sweetheart. Everything's going to be fine," he said, as if he were talking to the child, but his eyes were gazing directly into Laura's. He reached out and gently grasped her chin with his free hand, forming a bond between man and baby and woman. "I promise you, Laura, I give you my word, my solemn vow, that no one is going to question your actions anymore. I intend to see to that."

She shook her head slightly and her skin slid against his palm, sending warm curls of sensation through her body. Swallowing hard, she refused to look away from the determination in his beautiful, fierce blue eyes. "You can't force people to believe in me, Mick. You can't always be responsible for women in need. You can't fight my battles."

He skimmed his thumb across her bottom lip. "I'd place my body between you and anyone else that meant to harm you if it came to that, and you couldn't stop me from doing it, angel. I want you to know that you're not going through this alone. Like it or not, I'm involved. Stay home today while I find out what I can," he said.

But when he left a few minutes later, placing Meggie in her arms and brushing a light kiss over her forehead, Laura couldn't help worrying about the determined set of Mick's jaw.

Once again, he was coming to her rescue, like some hero out of a book. But books ended and heroes went home, she knew all too well, though the pain ripped through her at the thought.

And the rescued women went on alone, as they always had. They banded together to put bandages on their hurts. That's what she was going to attempt to do today. Worried as she was about her child and her future, she knew she wasn't the only woman hurting today. Megan Maitland hadn't called, and she had taken another blow this morning.

Laura couldn't just stand by and do nothing about that.

Like Mick, she had to act.

And it was the thought of Mick that drove her on as she climbed into her borrowed car and went in to work early. Mick had gone to battle for her so many times. It was time for her to be the strong one.

She thought about calling him to tell him she was leaving, but then she shook her head. The darn man would worry. He would probably decide to stick by her side for the whole day and then she would be of no use to anyone.

She would be with Mick, which would be... delicious.

"And all wrong, Maitland," she told herself. The key thing was to go help Megan and not to think about Mick and how she felt when he went all noble on her. Or how she felt when he gazed into her eyes and stroked her skin. Today was going to be difficult enough without aching for things she couldn't have.

She wondered if Megan would even let her work today. The woman hadn't called.

A lump of fear rose in Laura's throat. For herself, for Meggie, for Megan, too.

She wanted Mick badly at this moment.

But she forced herself to get ready for work, not knowing what would await her when she got there.

On the way to the day-care center, Laura flipped on a local station on the radio. Music streamed out into the car for a few minutes. It was soothing music, but she couldn't be soothed, and she was just about to punch the power button to Off when a voice broke in and the music died. The announcer reported that there would be an audio feed from a local television station, their sister station.

"This is an update from Blossom Woodward on the Maitland Maternity clinic situation." Blossom's voice poured into the small confines of the car. "I've just received a note, telling me that there's a third suspect in the Maitland Maternity clinic case. Hugh Blake is known to have his office in the area of the building where all the vandalism has occurred. Blake is an old and trusted associate of the clinic, and it's believed that he might have played a part in the recent activities. Earlier this morning, Megan Maitland made a brief statement in which she declared that the clinic was secure, that no patients have been endangered by the petty acts related thus far, and that Maitland Maternity clinic's internal security system would be handling the case. Still, this situation grows more interesting by the minute. The chief suspects are all either Maitland family members or trusted Maitland friends, and there's still no word on the whereabouts of Luke Maitland, our mystery Maitland of the moment. Blossom Woodward reporting for *Tattle Today TV*."

Laura's heart was pounding. Hugh Blake was now a suspect, too? A man whom Megan trusted heart and soul?

Her hands felt sticky on the wheel. She tried not to think about what would await her when she reached the clinic. She tried not to think about Luke at all, but where was he?

"Oh, Luke, come home," she pleaded. She needed the men she loved around her now, where she could make sure they were safe. Rafe and Luke and—

She refused to finish that thought, but she couldn't keep herself from looking for Mick as she entered the clinic, either.

He wasn't in sight.

Mick had been surveying what was going on at the clinic since he'd arrived, listening to the gossip that was circulating among his men and trying to make up his mind what would be the best course of action to help Laura.

After an hour of listening, he knew two things. The list of suspects was growing, and the local grapevine wasn't powerful enough when a man needed facts. He was going to have to wade into the heart of the Maitland family if he needed more news.

Turning quickly to head toward the wide doors of

the clinic, he thought he caught a glimpse of movement, not far behind him, eyes upon his back, but when he looked again there was nothing outside the usual hive of activity surrounding the completion of the clinic's addition.

"Watch it. You're getting jumpy, Hannon," he muttered under his breath. This was the second time lately that he'd had a sense that someone was watching him. Or watching Laura.

And that was the thought that held his attention. Because he was worried about her, he reasoned. Because she'd already met up with one scoundrel and now was somehow tangled with another who was involving her, intentionally or otherwise, in his dirty dealings. She made a man want to do all he could to keep her safe and happy. Any man, even a man who knew darn well he was bad news for her would care.

He probably should just stop thinking and go inside to try to discover which way the wind blew. He needed to explain to Megan that Laura would never hurt her.

Yeah, it was a plan that might yield some results. Megan had to be hurting with this recent talk about Hugh, but she was a reasonable woman and she saw with both her mind and her heart. She knew things about Laura that most people didn't know.

It was clear that most people didn't know much about much when he walked past the reception area on his way to find Megan's office.

"Hugh might have done it," one aide was whispering. "Could be. I mean, he's been sweet-talking Ms. Maitland for years. Maybe he saw that now that Clyde was back, his time had come and gone."

"Not Mr. Blake," her companion answered. "He adores Megan. But Laura, I just don't know. She seems nice enough, but then her sister had everyone fooled, too, didn't she?"

Mick turned his head. He aimed a deadly look at the two gossipy women.

They froze like rabbits caught snitching the farmer's lettuce. One of them finally opened her mouth. "We were just…"

The other one elbowed her. "Good morning, Mr. Hannon. Excuse me, we have work to do." And the two guilty-faced women scurried away down a hallway. He supposed he had no business being indignant. His own men were gossiping, and he had been listening. The only difference was that his men hadn't dared to say anything negative about Laura while he was within hearing distance.

So clear her name, he ordered himself. Find out what the circumstances are so that you can help her. *If* you can help her.

For a second, it occurred to him that he might not be able to do what was necessary, that he might fail Laura. What if the circumstantial evidence was too strong?

He practically snarled as he bumped into an aide hustling down a corridor, before he took a deep breath and excused himself.

Damn it all, he was losing it. And if he lost control, he'd be no good to Laura at all.

Mick forced himself to clear his thoughts. He continued on down the main corridor, trying to ignore the turnoff that led to the day-care center. Finally, he made it to Megan's office.

The young receptionist looked up at him and blew her bangs up out of her eyes. "I'm sorry, she's not here," she said wearily, in a tone that told him she'd been repeating the same line all day. "All I can tell you is that the security team is on top of things."

He smiled at her. "If she comes back, could you tell her that Mick Hannon would like to talk with her. It's about Laura Maitland."

At that, the woman sat up straighter. "Megan's just gone off to the day-care center to talk to Laura."

A slow alarm began to sound in Mick's brain. That wasn't right. He'd asked Laura to stay home.

And Laura had told him more than once that she had to fight her own battles. Didn't the woman have any sense of self-preservation at all?

It seemed that, no, she didn't, but he didn't have time to think about that. Backtracking down the hallway, Mick turned and made his way to the day-care center with as much haste as was possible without attracting attention.

He was almost to the entrance when he saw them. Laura and Megan and an unknown woman.

"She's not taking care of my kid," the woman said. "I know the stories about her. I work here, for heaven's sake, and I know what's going on here."

Megan stood up straighter. "Then you know more than any of us do, dear."

The woman raised her chin. "If she stole a painting, what might she do to a child?"

It was as if the woman had physically struck Laura.

Mick saw her flinch. She clenched her hand more tightly around Meggie's carrier so that she wouldn't drop her baby. He realized just how much was at stake here: Laura's reputation, her happiness, her future in which she would surely want to work with children, either as the nurse she wanted to be or in some other capacity.

It could all end here. Right this moment if something wasn't done.

Swiftly he came up behind the trio. He put his arm around Laura's shoulder. He had been planning on urging her to let him take her home, but now...

She jumped and looked up into his eyes, and her own were so green, so sad and frightened that he wanted to pull her into himself, into his body, into his heart. He wanted to keep her safe forever, but that wasn't an option. The best he could do was to go to bat for her now.

"What might she do to a child?" he asked softly. "You might ask me. I might know the answer to that, because I was with her when she spent hours walking the floor with her baby because Meggie was crying with a stomachache. She's a woman who cares deeply about the innocent and the unprotected. Her heart broke for that baby every time she looked at her. I understand your concerns, ma'am, but they're unfounded. She would harm herself before she'd harm your child. Absolutely. No question."

Laura looked at him with tears in her eyes. She smiled at him through those tears. "Are you sure you're not just posing as a construction worker?

Maybe you're really some knight rigged out in a hard hat and boots. Thank you, but…''

She turned to the young woman. "I would feel just as you do if I thought my baby was at risk. Wouldn't you, Megan?''

Megan sighed. Her hand shook as she patted Laura's arm. "We're all mother bears where our children are concerned, I guess. You'll have to do as you see best, my dear,'' she said to the young mother, "but I have to agree with Mick. I see her with these children every day. I watched her give birth to her own. She would go to the ends of the earth to save a child in peril, yours included. All of my employees are top notch, but I don't get many workers who feel that strongly about their jobs. She's just the kind of woman we need here during this time of stress. She's a soothing influence on the children, who seem to sense that something's gone astray in their world. Now, you go on home, and when all this is over, you come back and we'll talk.''

The woman looked at Laura. She seemed to hesitate. Then she opened her mouth. "I'm sorry,'' she said as her eyes misted over and she carried her son away down the hall.

For a few seconds no one spoke. Then Megan took a deep breath. "I'm sorry about that, too, my dear,'' she said.

"I could go home,'' Laura said, "if it would be easier for you here.''

"I meant what I told her. Stay. Everything seems to be getting so jumbled up and crazy lately. The babies sense it. We need you at the center and I'm needed in a meeting." Her body seemed to shrink, her eyes grew more sad.

Mick suspected that the meeting was about the theft of the painting and the note about Hugh. He wanted to assure her that everything would be all right, but that would have been a lie.

Something was very wrong.

The only thing he could make right concerned Laura. As Megan said goodbye and wandered back to her office, Mick carefully took Meggie's carrier from Laura and set the baby down on the thickly carpeted floor.

"Don't move, sweetheart," he told the baby with a quick smile.

Then he turned back to Laura, took her by the shoulders and sighed.

"Don't you ever listen?" he asked.

"I listened," she told him.

"And you ignored what I told you."

She shook her head. "I had to, Mick. I was worried about Megan. She loves Hugh, I think, and she's got a lot on her plate these past few days. When I came in the building this morning, I heard that she was going to arrange for Clyde Mitchum to see his son, Connor. That's got to be a worry to her, too."

He drew her close, not caring that they were in a public place, and laced his fingers behind her neck, tipping her head back.

"You can't save the world, sunshine," he told her.

"Isn't that my line?" she asked with a small sigh. "You can't save the world, either."

No, he couldn't, he thought. But he could possibly save the reputation of one woman.

"Go to work, then, if you have to," he whispered, kissing her lips lightly. "But promise me that you'll call Security if anything strange happens. Don't try to do anything on your own."

"I promise that much," she said. "If anything happened to me, Meggie would have no parents at all."

Her words broke his heart. She had obviously thought about that. She had known that in leaving her house today, she would be making herself a possible target and yet she had come. Because she thought Megan Maitland needed her to be here.

It was something to think about. She was risking a lot by being here today.

Several hours later, Mick made the decision to risk everything himself. Some new gossip had emerged about the theft of the painting. If it was true, he might have a solution as far as Laura was concerned. It would mean giving up on a few things himself, but then, was there anything he wouldn't do to clear Laura's name?

"No, there isn't," he muttered as he headed toward Ned to sign off. The move he was about to make would—hopefully—save the woman he was growing to care about, but it would also set off a small explosion within the Maitland family.

When this was over, not too many of the Maitlands would want to have him around, Laura included.

As he headed for his car, he saw Blossom Woodward leaving the clinic. She moved toward the parking lot, then glanced back over her shoulder as if there was someone behind her.

There wasn't.

But she took a few more steps, then whirled to face whatever she'd been looking for. She raised her head, like an animal breathing in the scent of its pursuer.

Finally, she turned back around, took three more steps and began running. She went to her car, flicked open the door, hopped in and sped off. The look on her face as she drove away was less that of a hard-boiled reporter and more like that of a woman who'd been terrified.

Mick glanced back in the direction she'd been looking. He slowly walked back toward the bushes that were tall enough to conceal a human being.

Unfortunately, this was a heavily trafficked area. Any footprints he might find could have come from anyone, and there was no one hiding there now.

Blowing out a breath, he retraced his steps.

"Nice going, Hannon," he muttered.

Blossom Woodward wasn't the woman who was invading his thoughts night and day of late, but right now she was the one woman he needed to see.

He would never have believed that he would be pursuing a television tabloid reporter, but then a few weeks ago he never would have believed that one woman, one small, green-eyed woman, could keep him aching twenty-four hours a day, either.

Chapter Ten

Laura had barely been home twenty minutes when Mick showed up at her door.

"How was work?" he asked her as soon as he'd gotten in the door. His voice was slightly strained. It was clear he wasn't anticipating good news.

"It was fine," she said, although that wasn't exactly the truth. The day had been stressful, but what could she have expected? The entire clinic was on edge and no one was clear as to who the enemy might be.

"Anyone else bother you?"

"Mick…"

He shook his head. "I promise I won't bust any heads or jump down the throats of any young mothers. I just need to know."

"All right, then," she said, crossing her arms. "Of course some people looked at me with suspicion. It's like one of those old movies where you suspect the traitor is one of your own, but you're not quite sure which person is the culprit. It wasn't easy for me, but it wasn't easy for anyone today, least of all for Megan. Actually, the rumor is that everyone is pretty convinced that Hugh is the guilty one, but what would his motives be? He has money. Why would he vandalize the clinic, and why would he steal a painting no matter how valuable?"

Mick held out his hands. "He's worked with the Maitlands for years. He might have issues, things no one really knows about, imagined slights even the Maitlands might not key into. These things happen all the time."

"I know," she said, "but it's hurting Megan so much."

"Come here," he said, and leaning back against the counter, he drew her to him.

"I know she cares for him. What must that be doing to her? To have not one man in her life, but two, betray her? And both in such major, dramatic ways? It's awful," Laura said, her voice small. She leaned into Mick, breathing in the scent of him, reveling in the warmth of his body.

Still pressed against him, she looked up into his eyes, which looked suddenly stricken. "Mick?"

He shook his head. "Men are scum sometimes," he said, his voice rough.

She smiled slightly and chuckled. "They sure are, but not all of them are, I guess. Some of them make up for the rest."

As he laid her cheek against his chest, his heart began to thunder. "Don't do that. You don't know much about me at all."

"So tell me."

But he simply stared down at her for a few long seconds. "I had a father who was a drunk, and he died and left my mother alone. I had a stepfather who was around when he wanted to be and not around the rest of the time. I don't have any interest in repeating history by marrying a woman and trying to be what I'm not cut out to be. Any woman who started thinking the wrong things about me might get hurt. I wouldn't want that to happen. After I'm gone, I want you to be happy."

Her throat started to close up. He thought she was asking him to stay, to care.

She pushed herself away. "I've been making my own happiness all of my life. Meggie and I have each other, and we'll have a good life together. Don't think otherwise." Her tone was breezy, but breezy was the last thing she felt.

"You'll be better if we get your bed in order," he said, his voice thick. "I'll put it together tonight."

And then he wouldn't have much reason at all to come around any longer.

"I'll make supper," she said, reiterating her original excuse for seeing him.

"Tomorrow I'll drive you to work," he said, as if he'd read her thoughts. "I know you're capable of getting around on your own, but there are things going on that no one quite understands."

She opened her mouth and he stopped her by putting one hand up.

"I'll rest easier knowing you're not crossing that

parking lot alone when the sun starts to set. I worried today.''

It was so simple, those three words, and yet her heart flipped over. He had worried today. It was unfamiliar territory, having a man who was not her brother worry about her. It was the kind of thing a woman could get used to when she shouldn't.

She didn't answer his request, and he slid one long, lean hand up her cheek. ''You could make a man crazy, Laura Maitland.''

And he kissed her. Just once. Long and hard. Then he gathered the pieces of the bed and his tools.

''We'll talk more later,'' he promised.

She busied herself at the kitchen counter, but behind her she could hear the sounds of her daughter cooing in her crib and the sounds of Mick sliding wood against wood.

When the doorbell rang, she turned, spaghetti-sauce-coated spoon in hand, but Mick was already moving toward the door.

He opened it and two men came in, carrying a blue-and-white mattress. They leaned it against the wall as he directed them, then left.

''You're not paying for that,'' she said, shaking her spoon at him.

He smiled. ''We'll talk later.''

Laura frowned. ''We'll talk now. I'm going to go get my checkbook. I have enough.''

''Laura?''

''What?''

''Hush, let me put the bed together.''

''And then you'll let me pay you?''

He didn't answer.

"Mick…"

"Laura?"

"Yes?"

"You're burning dinner. I think."

She sniffed, and while the darn man wasn't exactly right, he was close to it. Just in the nick of time, she turned down the burner and saved her sauce. "Men," she said, looking over her shoulder at him as she stirred, "are not to be trusted."

"That's right, darlin'. Don't ever forget that."

She swore she wouldn't, as she'd promised herself so many times in the past nine months, but when she turned around later after finishing the sauce and the spaghetti, Mick was tucking in the sheets he'd removed from her old bed. He flipped her emerald-green-and-cream comforter over the top and it floated down like a cloud, the perfect contrast to the golden wood of the new bed and the tiny frogs on the wallpaper. The room suddenly felt much more like a home.

"Oh, Mick, it's lovely," she said, turning off the stove and rushing over to smooth her palm over the golden curlicues of the bedposts. "It's a bed for a princess."

"Or a sleeping beauty," he said softly.

She looked up at him, smiling, knowing her heart was in her eyes. She had come to Austin, expecting only pain, and Mick had filled her life with a glow as golden as the wood of this gift he'd made for her.

She would lie here tonight and for all the nights that followed. Alone, while he went back to Dallas.

And she knew she would yearn for him, that she wanted to just once have a night with him on this bed.

When she looked into his eyes, she knew that he wanted it, too.

She took a step toward him. She held out her hand.

He moved forward, taking her hand and kissing the palm. His lips found her wrist. He kissed his way up the soft underside of her arm. When he reached her elbow, he raised his head. His eyes were dark.

"A man who would make a bed for a woman only so that he could lie with her on it would be the worst kind of heel, Laura."

She swallowed hard, she licked her lips and tried to find enough air to speak. "Even if that woman invited him into her bed?"

"Especially then," he said, taking her other hand in his and staring down at her ringless fingers. He kissed each one. "Because he'd never know if he made the bed out of the goodness of his heart or so that he could seduce the woman."

He slipped his hand behind the back of her neck then and drew her slowly to him. He kissed her with hunger and heat, tasting her over and over, making her mad with want.

She kissed him back, twisting so that her breath was his breath, her heartbeat was his heartbeat, and as they joined their bodies this way, she understood.

He thought he was a man like others she'd known, like his father and his stepfather. If they made love tonight, there'd be no convincing him otherwise.

She kissed him one last time, then pressed her palms to his chest, slowly levering herself away.

"Okay, you're right. This will have to be enough."

"This will never be enough," he said with a ragged voice.

But he stepped far away from her. Five minutes later, he left.

"He didn't even eat his dinner, hon," Laura said to Meggie. "I have a feeling I just pushed him away a bit further."

But at least tomorrow she would see him again. She would let him drive her to work as he'd asked. Not because she was worried about being in danger at the clinic, but because it was a pathetic excuse to spend a few minutes with the man who was beginning to mean too much to her.

"But this is Mick," she reasoned.

And Mick would never intentionally hurt her.

Mick pulled up in front of the Grand Villa Hotel and waited. Finally, he had tracked down his prey. It had taken a number of phone calls, a few bribes and a lot of waiting, but he'd finally run Blossom Woodward to ground. That was her car in the lot, all right.

He'd lost her last night after leaving the clinic. She hadn't gone home and she hadn't gone to the television station. Finally, he'd given up in disgust and stopped by Laura's to make sure that she was all right. Now, however, he was going to sit tight and outwait Blossom. The woman might be a pain, but right now she held the key to clearing Laura's name. He hoped.

Thirty minutes later, she finally emerged from the hotel, blond hair slightly mussed, dark glasses covering her eyes. She looked around warily, then headed for her car.

He stepped out of his.

The second she saw him, she stopped, looking as if she wanted to run. Then she crossed her arms.

"Are you the person who's been following me?"

"Not really. I'm the person who wants you to know the truth about Laura Maitland."

"What truth?"

"That she couldn't have stolen that painting."

"How do you know that?"

"I know, and I can provide proof."

She took her sunglasses off. Her eyes were alert. Slightly suspicious, but clearly interested.

"Tell me."

He raised one brow. "You'll run the story?"

"It depends on whether your proof will fly."

"No question."

She studied him as if she were assessing his honesty. He'd bet she'd heard a lot of lies over the years, but he didn't really care about the lies she'd been told. All he cared about was Laura.

Suddenly, she nodded. "Let's go into the restaurant," she said with a lift of her shoulders as she turned to walk back toward the hotel without waiting for him to follow. "We'll talk. I really need a cup of coffee."

So did he, but it wasn't what he needed most or even what he wanted most. Not that he had ever been likely to get what he wanted and needed. In coming to Austin, he'd simply intended to get to the bottom of a sticky situation. Now, with this move, he was unlikely ever to accomplish that goal.

No matter. For Laura's safety and happiness, he'd risk every goal he'd ever set for himself.

Laura was sending her last toddler off for the day with a hug and a wave goodbye to the child's mother when Mick came through the door of the day-care center.

The little curly-haired boy waved and smiled at him and Mick couldn't help grinning back. The kid's attitude was just infectious, and for the first time all day, the churning of his stomach eased a bit. He wondered if that was where Laura got her serenity in spite of all the turmoil surrounding her. She was forced to keep a smile on her face and to put aside her problems to deal with pint-size troubles. Spilled juice could seem like tragedy to a two-year-old. A skinned knee was more painful than anything when you didn't have much experience of wounds in your short life, he would imagine. So she shelved her worries, she dried tears with gentle fingers and soothing words. She rocked away her charges' troubles and sang songs to ease whatever woes had shattered a child's happiness. Putting her own interests aside, she waited, and her reward came in the form of sticky kisses, moist hugs and innocent smiles.

"He's cute," Mick said to Laura, almost stepping forward to claim his own kiss, then remembering where he was.

"He's spoiled rotten," she said with affection. "What a sweetie, though. You're early," she said suddenly, changing the subject and nearly catching him off guard.

Except he'd been expecting her to say that.

"Guilty," he said. "I've got something I want you to see."

She raised her brows. "What?"

"Don't worry, darlin'. It's nothing bad." He hoped. He desperately hoped this would turn out right. For her sake.

"Come with me," he continued. "There are others here who'll watch Meggie for a few minutes. We need a television set. The receptionist told me there was one in the employee lounge."

Instantly suspicion clouded her eyes. "More bad news?"

He shook his head. "Has it been difficult today?"

She clamped down on her lips, then shook her head as if to shake away whatever unpleasant things had happened today. "Not too bad. There's been such a tight lid on the information that's leaking out that people don't know what to think. Everyone's a bit nervous and jumpy.

"Lots of people didn't come in today. I don't know if it's because they're afraid something more might happen at the clinic or if they don't want to leave their children with me and have no other recourse. Megan seems heartbroken. She's determined to stand by Hugh and me, but Hugh didn't come in today. The only bright spot seemed to be when Connor came by to see her. He made his mother's day. I believe they were going to meet Clyde Mitchum for an early supper."

Mick nodded slowly, although his brain was on full alert now. "That worked out, did it?"

"I don't know, exactly," she said with a shrug, "but I took some of the children out for a walk later and I saw Clyde coming in the door. He seemed eager as a kid."

So maybe his stepfather *had* come here for all the right reasons, after all. The thought warmed Mick slightly, and he was able to smile.

"Come on, then. We'll check in on Megan later and make sure she got back all right and that she's okay." He took her elbow and began to steer her toward the door.

"I still don't understand why we need a television," she said.

"Humor me."

She nodded slightly and stepped inside the green-and-blue employee lounge when he opened the door. There was an unusually large number of people gathered there.

"Shh. They just announced that Blossom Woodward is going to be on with an update on the clinic situation," one woman said.

The rest of the people in the room glanced nervously at Laura, then turned their attention back to the television as if embarrassed to be caught watching something that could further implicate her.

"Mick, I don't think—" Laura's voice was weak. She stopped dead in her tracks.

He prayed this would work out the way he'd planned, but there was no time for further thought. Blossom's face appeared on the screen.

"Another puzzle piece in the never-ending puzzle of what is going on at the Maitland Maternity clinic. Laura Maitland, reputed to be a key player in the theft of a painting from the clinic, appears to have dropped off the list of suspects. After a careful analysis of the security tapes, the time of the theft has finally been determined. Today a witness, Mick Hannon, reported that he was with Laura at her house the night before last when the theft occurred. Her landlord, who lives on the same piece of property and who saw her in the window, holding her baby, has corroborated Mr. Hannon's story. But the questions still remain. Who has been attacking the clinic? And as for Luke and Janelle Maitland, where are you both tonight? More important, where will you show up next? Reporting from downtown Austin, Blossom Woodward for *Tattle Today TV*."

The broadcast ended. Someone pressed the off button on the remote and sudden silence filled the room. The battery-operated clock that hung over the table emitted a low hum and tick. A chair shifted and squeaked against the tile floor. Someone else coughed and cleared her throat.

An elderly nurse fussed with the lapels on the white jacket she was wearing.

"You didn't seem like a thief to any of us, Laura. It's just that well, Hugh Blake doesn't, either, and we've known him a long time. I'm sorry if any of us have been rude to you."

Laura stepped forward and touched the woman's hand where she was still fidgeting. "You haven't been rude, and it was only natural for people to wonder. A new person always takes some time to get used to, and under circumstances like these, who wouldn't be suspicious?''

Mick noticed that no one mentioned Luke or Janelle Maitland. He hoped no one would, and that this broadcast of Blossom's would make things easier for Laura at the hospital from now on.

As the two of them walked back along the corridors to find Meggie and get ready to go home, Laura stopped in an empty hallway and gazed up at him.

"Did you get any work done today at all?"

He shrugged. "Tons. This didn't take that long."

"Mick, how did you know that the timing was the same? No one's been releasing any information."

"Information always leaks out. The trick is being there when it spills over. I just made a point of listening to the right people."

"I'll bet you didn't think you were going to wade into this much trouble when you came to Austin."

He smiled slightly. "I've always been partial to trouble. Makes life more interesting."

"I must be making your life incredibly interesting, then."

"You are. You have." He couldn't keep the low thrum out of his voice, and her eyes widened slightly.

"Have you—" Her own voice broke. She shook her head and tried again. "Have you had a lot of trouble in your life?"

He knew what she was asking him. She meant had he had any other woman he'd spent this much time looking out for. He hadn't, but he didn't want to tell her that. It would mean too much, then, and neither of them could afford for any of this to mean too much.

"Trouble has tailed me all my life," he said, which was the truth. Just not the whole truth. "It's a gift, I guess." And he grinned to show her that she shouldn't feel self-conscious or worry that he resented any time he'd spent on her.

She stared into his eyes for several seconds, long enough that he wanted to lean forward and kiss away her concerns and had to fight his instincts.

Finally, she shook her head.

"Maybe so, but I get the feeling that your life is going to be a lot more restful after you go back home."

Mick didn't even want to think about what it would be like to go back home, even though he was going. No reason to stay now. Dell needed him more in Dallas than Ned needed him here.

And Laura? Well, after today, she probably didn't need him at all.

It was a good thing, no doubt, but it was still something that made him want to tuck her and Meggie into his truck and take them back home with him.

Just for a few weeks, of course.

Silly thought. His work here was done. Clyde appeared to be taking the high road and his stepson wasn't needed here, anymore.

A few minutes later, Mick and Laura carried Meggie out the door of the clinic.

Clyde Mitchum was waiting for them, and he was not a happy man.

Chapter Eleven

Mick looked at the set line of Clyde's jaw, the way his body quivered as he and Laura drew near. It looked like the game was already up. He'd been hoping for a bit more time, but no matter. Time wasn't really going to make any difference.

"Mick, aw, Mick, I can't believe you did this to me," Clyde said, pacing back and forth across the asphalt. "To think that here I was, working day and night to get my life back on track, to right the wrongs I'd done to that dear woman, finally trying to do some good for once in my life, and you came here in secret, because you didn't trust me to act like a man. Tell me that you came here for some other reason. Please, son."

Clyde's voice cracked, and for a moment, Mick felt a sense of deep regret. "I came here to look out for you," he said. He'd always had a soft spot for this old man who hadn't always been much of anything resembling a father. "I'm here because I cared."

"If you cared, you would have let me know you were in town. You didn't trust me."

Well, there was no denying that. He *did* care what happened to Clyde, but...well, no, he didn't always trust him.

"Deny it. Please deny it, Mick," Clyde said, his voice quivering slightly. "You're the only son I ever really knew."

Mick looked up at the sound of tears gathering in Clyde's voice.

"It hurts me, Mick. It does, my boy. So much. Right here, son." And Clyde thumped his chest, hard.

Ah, the old Clyde. He meant well. Mick prayed the man meant well, but he had just always hammed it up a bit too much. It had spoiled the cons he'd tried to run. It had made people suspect him. That sense of drama had gone straight to Maeve's heart and sometimes it had hurt her.

Mick spared a glance for Laura and saw that her eyes were troubled and bleak. She knew now that he was as big a con man as his stepfather was. He was a liar, a man who lied by omitting all the facts. It hurt too much to look at her, and, anyway, what could he say that wouldn't just hurt her even more? He turned back to Clyde.

"I wish things could have been different," he said to his stepfather, but he knew his words were really for Laura.

"Are you telling me that your purpose in being here in Austin wasn't to follow me, Mick?" Clyde asked.

But he couldn't lie when the game was all over. "Maeve loved you so much," he said gently. "I promised I'd look after you."

"You should have trusted me."

"Should I have, Clyde?"

The man had the good grace to draw himself up slightly and shake his head. "I've done wrong in my life, Mick. Many times. But I did care for your mother. I care for you, too."

It was Mick's turn to shake his head…because he didn't really know whether Clyde told the truth or whether he lied. But there had been a day long ago when Clyde had taken a troublesome young teenager fishing when he probably would have rather gone drinking with his buddies. And he had held Maeve's hand as she died. He'd wept bitter tears.

"You're a tough man to love, Clyde," Mick said gently. "A tough man not to love, too, and yes, I'm here to look after you. I've been following you. I'm not going to apologize for it, since I'd do the same again."

Clyde stared back at him for long moments. Then, finally, he shook his head. "Every man has to do what he's called to do, I suppose, Mick. I have my own calling, you know."

Mick nodded. "I wasn't trying to hurt you, Clyde, but perhaps I should have handled this situation differently."

"You could have simply asked me what I was up to."

Shrugging, Mick smiled slightly and tried not to laugh. "Would you have told me the whole truth?"

"Every man deserves to keep some secrets."

"Sometimes keeping secrets can be considered the same as telling a lie. Still, I apologize if I hurt your feelings, Clyde. You'll be happy to know I'm going back to Dallas the day after tomorrow. As soon as I tie up some loose ends. I do actually have a job here. It's not all been spying on my stepfather."

Clyde nodded. He grumbled. Finally, he held out his hand. "I'll call you one day soon," he said. "Take care of yourself."

And then he turned and bowed slightly to Laura. "My apologies, ma'am. We shouldn't be airing our dirty laundry in public," he said, nodding toward a few people who had paused to stare. "Definitely not in front of you."

"I understand," Laura said, and her voice was faint.

Oh, hell, what had he done, Mick thought, as Clyde walked away.

He had come here to spy on Clyde Mitchum. He was Clyde Mitchum's stepson. The words spun round and round in Laura's head as she placed Meggie in Mick's truck, climbed in the front seat and waited for Mick to drive away.

She could feel his eyes on her, but she couldn't look at him. She just couldn't.

"Laura?"

Slowly, she shook her head. "Not yet," she whispered. "Could you take me home now, please?"

Silence hung in the air for several seconds. Then Mick started the truck and moved out into the traffic.

Tears began to mist up in front of her eyes, and

Laura fought them. She clenched her fists as if it would help. She turned her head to the side and looked out the side window when she began to lose the battle.

Finally, Mick drew up in front of her apartment. He started to get out of the truck.

"No," she said, her voice thick and almost unintelligible through her tears. "No, we can get in just fine. Really."

"Laura, we need to talk."

And somehow she mastered herself. She blinked back her tears and looked at him. "No, we don't," she said quietly. "Mick, you don't need to tell me anything. You've been so good to us, such a help. I don't know what we would have done without you, but Meggie and I need to start thinking about getting on with our lives now. We really do. Already, I'm afraid she's starting to listen for the sound of your voice. That's just not good. You have things to do, and so do I. We've had this time while you did your job and looked out after your stepfather, but now, I just—well, I can't think straight tonight. All right?"

He stared down into her eyes, his own blue ones dark and filled with concern.

"I should have told you the truth all along," he said softly.

Vehemently, she shook her head. "Like Clyde said, we all have things we're called to do. I know that if you didn't tell me the truth about why you were here, you had good reasons. We both need to realize that this is almost the end. Don't you think so?"

And what could he say? She was practically begging him not to hurt her any more. He had, essentially, lied to her, and she was a woman who had been lied to too many times in her life. If he said that he didn't want to end this, that would be a lie, too, when he had nothing to offer her. And she would know it for the lie that it was.

She was right. They'd pushed this further than either of them ever would have expected, and further than they should have.

He leaned across the seat of his truck, reached out and slid his hand down her cheek, thumbing away a lone tear that trickled down her pale skin.

"You're right. It's almost the end. I'll be going back to Dallas early the day after tomorrow. Will you be all right tonight?"

"I'll be all right tonight and beyond. Survival is something the Maitland women are good at." Her eyes were dark with pain and determination. She nodded, and her damp skin slid against his palm.

He thought he just might remember the feel of her skin against his palm for the rest of his life. He thought something else, too.

I love her. The thought edged in, scaring him to death. He loved her, and there was no question in his mind that he had lost her trust. He'd kept secrets. He'd been like so many others in her life.

That was going to have to change now. But how? Why should she believe in him after today?

Laura stepped into her house several hours later and slid slowly down to seat herself, back against the door. She held Meggie in her arms. Her landlord had run across not long ago and insisted she come watch his television. Her young man was on the screen.

It hadn't been her young man. "We don't have a young man, do we, sweetie?" she asked, kissing her daughter's fluffy hair. It had been Mick.

"That Blossom works fast, doesn't she, Meggie?" She'd obviously heard all about the confrontation between Mick and Clyde. No surprise since it took place right in front of the clinic. No surprise that she'd rushed a special story on about them, either. Clyde's failures of the past had been paraded out again, and speculation about what kind of man would spy on his stepfather had played a generous part in the story. Anyone who didn't know Mick would assume that he was shifty, maybe even a bit mean, a liar.

Laura flinched at that last thought. He *had* lied to her, or at least he hadn't told her the whole truth, but he had done so much more, too. And he hadn't really had any obligation to tell her what his personal business here in town was, had he? If she'd been hurt by his failure to trust her that much, well...it wasn't a very grown-up way for her to act. She and Mick were just two people who had shared some extraordinary experiences. That was all.

"I shouldn't be thinking bad things about him, and neither should anyone else." A memory of what it was like to have people staring disapprovingly at her and her mother rose up unbidden. Her mother had tried to shield her from those looks, but it never had worked.

"Hold up your head, baby," Veronica had said, and Laura had tried. But it still hadn't taken away the sting of those looks, or worse, the meaning of the hushed and slurred whispers people had cast her way.

The thought of Mick picking up his phone innocently or stepping outside his door unprepared, only to be greeted with that kind of venom, came to her. He wouldn't even mention it to her, if that happened, she was sure of that. Perhaps she should invite him over here, so that he could be away from the calls and the knocks on his door. Once people learned that he was Clyde Mitchum's son and he had been working incognito right outside Maitland Maternity, there was bound to be harsh talk.

She picked up the phone and quickly dialed Mick's number. It rang and rang and rang. He'd gone out— or maybe he hadn't, and he had simply stopped answering his phone.

That thought nagged at her. A feeling of impotence settled in. She felt the need to move, to act, to help Mick.

"There must be something we can do. He deserves so much better, sweetie, don't you think?" she asked Meggie.

It seemed to Laura that Meggie's slight baby cooing was a sound of approval. She carefully rose with her child, placed Meggie in her crib, and moved back to the phone once again.

One hour later, Blossom Woodward was staring around Laura's apartment. She kept looking into the corners as if something was going to materialize.

"So you're telling me that Mick Hannon isn't just some man you're dating?" Blossom finally asked. She looked down to scribble Laura's expected response, oblivious to the way her comment affected Laura, who sat up straighter.

"We're not d-dating at all," Laura stammered. "Maybe you thought that because of what Mick told you about his being here with me the night the painting was stolen."

Blossom looked up at her, her eyes darting around the edges of the room again. Finally, she took a long, deep breath and smiled slightly. "Maybe I thought that because the man was more than ordinarily perturbed that anyone should say anything negative about you, Laura. The man is clearly smitten."

Laura blinked her eyes. Well, even she wasn't going to deny that there was something physical that Mick felt for her, but...

"It's not like that," she insisted. "And that's not what I wanted to talk about. Mick is special. It's true that I don't know that much about him, but I know that he's a decent man. He came here to keep an eye on his stepfather because he knew of Clyde's connection to the Maitlands. He ended up helping me, a Maitland woman, deliver my baby. And it didn't end there. He's kept an eye on us, looked out for our safety, and even gone so far as to correct your story. He's a good man."

Blossom nodded. She looked much more nervous than she usually did on television. She was an attractive woman, but her eyes had dark shadows beneath them. "Hon," she finally said, "good men, unfortunately, make boring TV, but that bit about the mystery man with a distant connection to the Maitlands being called on to save a Maitland woman in distress, now, that's something different. It's the kind of thing viewers eat up and ask for more. And with a man that looks like Mick, well, let's just say I'll be glad to dig in a little deeper on this one. I'll run it in the morning on my regular broadcast.''

Laura breathed a sigh of relief. She started to rise, but Blossom placed a hand on hers to stop her. This time Blossom looked even more nervous. Her hand was cold.

"Laura, what can you tell me about your brother? What kind of man is Luke?"

Laura raised her chin. "You've asked me about Luke before. Are you trying to pin something on him?"

Blossom hesitated. "I—"

"I'm not going to tell you anything that might hurt him."

"So you know where he is? Is he here?"

"Why would you ask that? Because of the theft and the vandalism?"

Blossom hesitated. Her hand tensed on Laura's. Finally, she sighed. "I've been asking a lot of questions about Luke, and now I think I'm being followed. It could be Janelle, but... I wondered—I'm asking you as one woman to another—do you think your brother might be dangerous?"

The implications of what Blossom was asking seeped into Laura's being. The absolute fear the woman had been going through was clear in the tension of her icy fingers against Laura's own.

"I love my brother ferociously," she said solemnly, staring at Blossom. "He's a good man, but he's also complicated. He wouldn't hurt a woman. You should know that, but..."

"But?"

Laura swallowed. "He might well follow a woman if he thought that woman meant to hurt someone he cared about."

Slowly, Blossom eased up on Laura's hand. She cleared her throat. "I wonder if that's meant as a threat."

"No. It just means that while Luke is a good man, he isn't going to let you get too close if he doesn't want you to."

Blossom seemed to digest that, but now with the edge off her fear, her eyes had taken on a hint of the speculative sparkle she was noted for. "I'll keep that in mind," she said as she left.

It was clear that Laura hadn't deterred her from her purpose where Luke was concerned. She hoped that the story Blossom would run about Mick would clear Mick's reputation with those in Austin who were starting to eye him with distrust after this evening's broadcast.

"So why'd I do that, Meggie?" she asked her daughter softly as the baby lay sleeping in her moon-dusted bed.

The answer to that was too obvious. She loved him. She had become her mother, willing to give all for a man who couldn't promise her a thing.

"And the day after tomorrow he'll be gone," she whispered to the pale sheen of the moon. She would have to say goodbye.

Tomorrow was going to be the worst. She'd have a whole day to think about Mick leaving.

Mick glanced at the package on the passenger seat of his car and considered chucking it out the window. He felt like a kid going to his first dance and showing up at the door with a corsage that was too big or too small or the wrong color.

He wanted everything to be perfect, and nothing was perfect. Tomorrow morning he was going back to Dallas. He was leaving Laura with the knowledge that she had been right all along. Men just weren't to be trusted. They breezed into a woman's life, stayed awhile, and then moved on. No point in putting your faith in such an irresponsible creature. Definitely no point in offering such a fly-by-night something as precious as a woman's heart.

For two seconds he wanted to pick up the package and fling it out the window. A gift, especially such a nothing of a gift, did not make up for not being the kind of man Laura needed a man to be.

"Yeah, well, you knew from the start that you weren't fit for her. Let's just get this day over with and then pack your bags and head back home."

Home. As if he had one. Maeve was long gone. There was no one but Dell waiting for him in Dallas.

"And no one here, either, idiot. She told you all along she didn't want a husband. Not that you could ever be one."

He slammed his hand against the steering wheel, forced himself not to think, and made it to Laura's apartment in record time. It was amazing that there wasn't a line of policemen on his tail, since he couldn't for the life of him remember stopping at stop signs or signaling turns.

For ten seconds he just sat there, staring up at Laura's window, memorizing what it was like to pull up and anticipate spending a few minutes with her. This would be the last time he'd do this. By the time he brought her home tonight, it would be getting dark, and besides, he didn't intend to do more than make sure she made it safely inside her door at the end of the day. If he came inside tonight, the knowledge of all that he would never share with her would hit him. He might end up touching her, taking her if she'd have him, and leaving her right where she'd been when he found her, sliding pregnant on the pavement into some other man's arms.

"Hell." So much for not thinking. Mick shoved open his door and started to climb out of his truck. At the last minute, he turned back and looked at the tacky little package. He scooped it up, slipped it in the pocket of his shirt and slammed the door closed.

Tromping up the outside stairs leading to her place, he found the door open when he reached the top. Laura stood in the doorway, her green eyes wide and full of questions. She held out her hand to pull him inside. She bit down on her lip nervously.

"Are you all right?" she asked. "I was worried after I saw Blossom's broadcast last night. I tried to call, but there was no answer."

"I'm sorry, angel. I didn't even see last night's broadcast. Clyde called and asked to see me again. He told me that, in spite of everything, Megan has decided to finish what she's set in motion. Connor is letting him meet with Chase and her today. After that, they'll see. I guess he just wanted to make sure that I wouldn't interfere.''

And Laura's eyes filled with relief. ''So, you didn't see the broadcast. That's okay. It wasn't worth watching.''

That bit of light that turned her face from distressed to beautifully ecstatic turned a key in his soul, and suddenly he knew something he hadn't known until this minute.

''I heard about the broadcast, though,'' he said slowly, ''and I saw this morning's *Tattle Today TV*. Seemed funny that Blossom should run a critical show on me last night and then present me as some sort of intriguing saint this morning. I wonder who told her all those nice things about me.''

A sweet sweep of pink climbed Laura's neck and colored her cheeks. ''Anyone who knew you might have told her.''

''Not that many people around here know me very well.''

She raised her chin in that adorable way she had. ''More than you think. The day I talked to your men, I got the distinct impression that they thought you were personally responsible for making the stars shine every night.''

''Maybe, but I doubt they would have included that part about me holding your hand all during labor. Not a guy thing, darlin'.''

She shifted and turned her head away slightly.

''I'm on to you, sweetheart,'' he said softly. ''I

don't suppose you'd believe me if I told you that you didn't have to put yourself on the line like that. I've faced criticism before.''

She whirled back and now there was budding anger in her eyes. "So have I, but that wouldn't have made it right for people to be angry at you when you were only looking out for your stepfather.''

"Pretty sure my motives were pure, aren't you?''

That chin tilted slightly higher. She was magnificent when she was indignant. Just watching her bloom before him made him want to step closer, crowd her a little, touch his lips to that sweet little pulse in her throat, then drag her closer and taste the wine and roses of her lips. He wanted to kiss her until she grew soft and hungry in his arms. He wanted to take her to bed so that they could both find out what heaven was really like, once and for all.

But he wouldn't.

"I'm sure you had good reasons for doing what you did,'' she finally said.

It was good that she was sure, because he sure as hell wasn't sure about anything. Not about his motives concerning Clyde, and definitely not about anything he'd done where Laura was concerned. He'd been in fifty feet of dangerous water from the get-go, and losing badly all the way. It was a good thing he was on his way out of here early tomorrow. Otherwise he might do something incredibly stupid and irrevocable, and she might be the one to pay the price for his mistakes.

"That was sweet,'' he said, brushing her nose with the tip of one finger, and trying to go for the flippant, friendly approach that was surely the wisest thing to do. "Thank you. I don't think I've ever had anyone set out to champion me before. Kinda nice."

She blinked at his tone. She sucked in a deep breath. "Well," she said slowly, "I only hope it helped."

"It helped me to know that you did it," he said softly. "You and no one else." And he realized he was slipping right out of friendly and heading toward loverlike. "I'd better get you and Meggie to the day-care center," he added, his voice going rough.

He stood up straighter and headed toward Meggie's crib where she was busy studying her toes.

"Come on, sweet stuff," he said, picking her up easily, as if he'd been born to do so. He tried not to think about the fact that this was probably his last opportunity in life to breathe in her baby powder scent or feel those tiny sticky fingers pulling at his face in newborn amazement. "Come on, hon, all the other babies are probably waiting for you. The show can't start without you being there. Probably lots of little boy babies waiting for this little pink blanket of yours to come through the door."

Trying to smile through his sense of loss, he turned with his prize and stared into Laura's stricken eyes.

"She'll miss you," she whispered.

"Honey, she's a baby."

"But—"

"She won't even know I'm gone," he said. "Years from now, I won't even be a memory."

The truth hit him like a giant steel fist. He kept moving toward Laura.

Finally she nodded tightly, then picked up Meggie's

diaper bag. Together they moved out the door like a married couple with their child.

Except they weren't that.

They were a couple who had been thrown together by circumstance, and now life was returning them to the way it was supposed to be.

As they drove toward the clinic, the silence felt like a huge cloud holding them apart, but what was there to say? He was going. She was staying. Their lives would part paths when he left town tomorrow morning and would never cross again.

"I'll make it clear to everyone that you didn't know of my connection to Clyde," Mick said suddenly. It had just occurred to him that the Maitlands might think Laura had been aware of more than she had been.

She placed her hand on his where it rested on the seat between them, and Mick almost closed his eyes and swerved the car. He fought for control.

"Don't worry about me, Mick. I can take care of myself, but if it will make you feel better, I promise I'll talk to Rafe if I need anything."

He took his eyes off the road to look at her. "It makes me feel a lot better, but just so you know, I've already mentioned to him that he might want to take over driving you to and from work."

She opened her mouth. To protest, he was sure. He shook his head and pulled into the clinic's lot. "I know you're capable, Laura, but these are difficult times. Just promise me you'll let your brother do this until they catch whoever is causing all the trouble at the clinic."

For a second, Laura hesitated. Then she slowly nodded. "All right. Blossom Woodward thinks she's being followed."

"I know. I didn't want to scare you."

"I'm not scared for me. Blossom's the one who's being followed."

Mick refrained from mentioning that day outside Laura's apartment. No need to if she was taking precautions.

"I'm agreeing to Rafe taking me home, so that if you hear anything on the television about what's going on here, you won't worry," she said softly.

As if the day would ever arrive when he wouldn't worry. He was going to die worrying about her. But she wouldn't want to know that.

He smiled at her. Not much of a smile, but one that counted. "Rafe and I thank you. It's tough for him walking that thin line between wanting to help you and wanting to let you do what you need to do. It's tough for any man." Just as if he felt nothing more for her than any other man did. "Come on, let's get you inside."

She eased her hand away from his and busied herself getting her daughter out of the car.

He walked her all the way to the day-care center today. He didn't explain. She didn't ask for explanations, but at the door, she turned to him. "You probably need to get on with things. You don't have to come back for me tonight. I'll call Rafe," she promised, with just a little catch in her voice.

Desolation swept through him. Denial. "We'll end as we began," he said. "I'll take you home. I have things to finish up here with Ned, anyway, and that will take most of the day.''

"All right, then. Goodbye, Mick.''

Not yet, he thought. We still have tonight, a few minutes more. But that would sound desperate. That would sound like the words of a man who had fallen so hard for a woman that he couldn't bear to be away from her even for a few minutes. She would know he needed her, but she didn't want to need anyone. How could he burden her with what was in his heart? How could he ever hope to be worthy of her?

He turned to go, then slowly pivoted back. "I almost forgot,'' he said, sliding the small package from his pocket.

She looked up in amazement, as if no one had ever given her a present. He wondered if she'd gotten many, considering how poor she'd been as a child. He'd been poor, too, but Clyde had liked to hand out things. He'd liked to play the part of the magnanimous head of the household.

"It's nothing much,'' he whispered. "Not even a very good match. And it's not meant to be a substitute. I just thought—well, if yours ever crumbled entirely, you'd have nothing of her. No reminders. That's all it's meant to be. I'll see you at the end of the day, love.''

The word slipped out.

Laura's breath came out on a gasp. He didn't apologize. "We'll say goodbye when I see you then,'' he added, so that she wouldn't think his endearment meant that he was asking anything of her. He would never ask anything she didn't want to give. Even if he wanted to get down on his knees and beg.

For once in his life, he wished with all his heart that he was the kind of man who knew that when he said he would be a good husband, he would be just that. He wanted to try, but if he took the risk and failed, she would be the one to suffer.

Not an option, he thought as he left her there and went off to start cutting the rest of his ties here. Hard to believe that by this time tomorrow, Austin and Laura would just be a part of his past.

Chapter Twelve

"Are you all right, Laura?" Beth Maitland's voice was filled with concern. She stared at the phone Laura had hung up only minutes before. "I heard that your sister was arrested and taken into custody. Would you like to go home early?"

Laura shook her head. "Thank you, but no. The children and the center keep me grounded. I feel at home here, and anyway, it's sad to say, but Janelle and I were never close. I don't think she ever even liked me, and I guess I feel as if I never really knew her at all. I can't even begin to understand what kind of a woman would kidnap a baby."

But she understood other things, Laura couldn't help thinking later that day as she said goodbye to her last parent and child and moved to the window to stare at the sky, which was slowly fading from sunny to gray.

An ache, so deep she could barely keep breathing,

filled her soul. The day was over, or nearly over. There was nothing left to do but ride home with Mick and watch as he climbed in his truck and drove away from her for the last time. Nothing left to do but end what she had started with Mick in this very place a month earlier.

Not that it was a day of endings for everyone. Clyde and Megan had left the clinic with Chase, their grandson, in tow several hours ago.

Rafe was still here. He'd called Laura to make sure she was okay after he'd heard about Janelle, and even Blossom was still in her life. She'd called to thank Laura for being so open and honest.

"In my line of work, I don't get many people who open up to me," she'd admitted. "If you don't mind, I'd—well, I'd like to bring a little something by for your baby today. It's the kind of thing I never get to do, all that girl stuff, and I'm guessing you didn't really have time for much of a shower."

Her voice had been filled with such eagerness and friendship that Laura had been happy to say yes. The truth was that if she weren't so distraught about Mick right now, she'd be looking forward to seeing Blossom. Maybe someday the two of them would be friends, but today...

Today she waited for Blossom to show up and for the hands of the clock to slip round to the hour when Mick would arrive and end their time together....

"I don't want it to end," she whispered to herself, clutching the small angel figurine in her hand. Blue and white and gold, it wasn't really like the one her mother had cherished, and yet...

"It was so like the man to go and do something so caring," she said. "To give me something to remember my mother by."

But of course, every time she looked at the pale blue figure, it would be Mick she'd be thinking of and longing for.

Her heart cracked in two, but she held back her tears. He would hate himself if she cried. He'd never forgive himself if he thought he was responsible for any pain on her part.

Laura fought to control herself. She gazed out the window where darkness was settling in heavily and the lights were just coming on.

Seeing out into the darkness wasn't easy, but— there, surely that was Blossom pulling up and climbing from her car. And who was that she was talking to? Someone in black. A groundskeeper? Laura couldn't really tell through the glare of the glass and with the man's back turned. She could see Clyde and Megan and Chase returning, though. The trio had just stepped into the glow of the bright entrance lights. Clyde was herding his charges toward the clinic doors.

Laura was just about to move away from the window toward the front of the day-care center to wait for her new friend when Blossom leaned into the revealing glow of a decorative light. She was looking down toward the groundskeeper, who must have said something, because Blossom tilted his way as if to catch his words, but at that moment, the man dove for her.

A muffled crack—one, two, three—split the silence,

followed by screams and yelling. Blossom's, Megan's, Clyde's.

In the light and shadow through the glare of glass, Laura thought she saw the groundskeeper rise and pull a gun. He fired into the night, then pulled Blossom to her feet and began to run, dragging her along, straight toward the edge of the parking lot.

A truck was at the curb, its dark surface gleaming in the parking lights. The man ducked and climbed inside, hauling Blossom in behind him as another shot pinged on metal. A split second later, the truck roared to life and shot down the drive at top speed.

Laura realized she had covered her mouth to hold back a scream. Her mind replayed the strobelike seconds that had just passed. The result was still the same. Blossom was gone.

And somewhere outside the hospital there was a gunman on the loose. Clyde and Megan were on the grounds.

And where was Mick, who always worked outside?

She had to get out there.

"Call 911 and tell them there's a man with a gun on the grounds. And stay with Meggie, Beth, please," Laura called, dropping her ceramic angel and bolting for the door.

Mick! Her soul seemed to scream his name. Her heart stopped beating completely at the thought that he might have been in the line of fire. Then it shot to life again with a rapid-fire explosion. She had to get to him.

Laura took the stairs. She flew down corridors, slid around turns and sprinted for the front doors.

She ran full-tilt out into the night and the glare of the lights as she turned her head from side to side, looking for the man she loved—and seeing nothing of him.

Clyde and Megan were moving slowly toward the doors. Clyde was limping. His face was ashen. His arm was around Megan and Chase. Megan's stockings were torn.

A small crowd of those who were still at work had tumbled out of the hospital and people were running through the night. Crying. Screaming. Faces looked shell-shocked. Eyes wore the signs of horror.

Gunfire at Maitland Maternity? This was not like a painting being stolen. This was life and death and terror.

Laura stumbled forward and hugged Megan and Chase close.

"Are you all right?" she whispered.

Megan tried to nod, but her head barely moved. "Clyde saved us," she said. "I heard the bullets whistling, but he pushed us down and covered us."

Tears sluiced down her face, and down Laura's.

The scream of the crowd was getting louder. The swarms of onlookers were swelling as cell phones appeared and word spread.

A television truck came roaring up. Even before the police arrived, Laura mused.

The crowd jostled. Megan, small and invisible in this throng, got shoved and Clyde tried to protect her.

Someone ran past Laura and whirled her around.

She opened her mouth, and felt a moment of horror herself. Where was Mick? Was he hurt? Was he down on the ground somewhere? Bleeding? Unconscious, perhaps? Was he…gone like Blossom? He'd been late. Had there been a reason? A bad reason?

Pain and fright rose within Laura like a silent scream.

The sound of a woman's hysterical sobbing drifted in.

Someone else pushed—and then shoved. An angry yell broke in.

"All right, everyone, let's take it easy and keep calm," a low, commanding voice said over the buzz of the crowd. "Go back inside. By being out here, you're only endangering yourself and the lives of others."

Mick's voice flowed through Laura like a rich, healing balm. She looked up to see him standing on the hood of his truck, above the din of the crowd.

"The police are on their way right now," he repeated, his voice firm and in command. He was staring right into Laura's eyes, freezing her in place. "They need to be able to do their job. You need to give them room to do that. Unless you were out here when the shots were fired, I want you to go back inside where you can wait safely."

The crowd looked up at him as if mesmerized by the sound of his voice, as if drawing strength from being near him.

"Please, you're endangering Megan and other innocents," Mick said slowly, as if he were speaking to a crowd of children. "She's here, and she needs your cooperation," he urged, and finally people began to break away. The crowd began to part.

Laura stood there, her eyes on Mick as he jumped down from atop his truck and started to move toward her, his stride long-limbed and purposeful.

"Laura," he said, his voice breaking.

Then he was running. His blue eyes were achingly fierce. They warmed her and chased away the iciness of fear.

She took a faltering step forward, and he bore down on her, catching her up in his arms.

"Laura, love, I thought I'd go stark raving crazy when I couldn't find you. As soon as I heard the shots, all I could think of was getting to you."

Laura looked up, tears in her eyes. "I was afraid you might have gotten hit by those bullets," she managed to choke out. "I don't think I could have survived that." Her voice was a broken whisper. She pressed into him and he lifted her against his heart.

"As soon as I heard that a woman was taken, I called upstairs. I didn't think I could even speak, I was so damn scared that it was you. And then, when they told me that you'd run out, I—"

His voice broke, and he clutched her tighter. He pulled back just far enough so that he could see her face.

"I have to kiss you," he whispered fiercely. "I need to know that you're real and that you're alive."

Laura slid her arms up between them and around his neck. She rose on her toes. "We're alive," she whispered back. And she lifted her lips for his touch.

He covered her mouth with his own and the world spun away, the people remaining outside the clinic disappeared, only to return when Mick finally pulled back and away from her.

"You're sure you're okay?" he asked softly, his voice weaker than she ever remembered hearing it.

She nodded tightly, then flinched at the sound of shoes scraping on the pavement. She'd all but forgotten Megan and Clyde.

"Megan?" she asked.

"We're fine, dear," the woman said. "Just a little shaken up. You and Mick go find your baby."

It took a couple of hours, however, before the police had taken statements, examined the scene and allowed them to go. Mick pulled up in front of her apartment and carried Meggie inside. He eased her out of her carrier, placed her in her crib. He began to pace. Like a lion in a pen that's too small, he crossed the room back and forth.

Laura watched him. She zeroed in on those dark and dangerous eyes of his. She noticed everything about him, the way he stole peeks at Meggie and then tried to pretend that he hadn't even noticed her, the way he looked at her with anguish in those deep blue eyes.

He cared. But he was a man who cared deeply about others, too. He had kept secrets and spied on his stepfather in order to protect Clyde and the Maitlands. He was simply a man who cared too deeply about the welfare of others.

If she loved him so much, she should put him out of his misery and send him on his way.

"Mick?"

The time had come to set him free and break her heart.

Mick looked down at the woman who held his heart in every way. She walked toward him slowly, each step bringing her closer.

He wanted her closer.

She touched him, boldly, her hand resting on his sleeve. He closed his eyes and felt the splay of her fingers against his skin, her warmth through the cloth, her essence joining with his.

"I know you have to leave," she said, and though her touch was sure, her voice was a bit unsteady and weak.

He wanted to drop to his knees, clutch her to him and ask her to stay with him forever.

Instead, he simply gazed down at her. He raked his knuckles across the soft skin of her cheek.

"I have to go," he agreed, his words not much more than a whisper.

She dragged in a deep, shaky breath. He leaned closer to her, inhaling the soft scent of flowers that he'd never forget in this lifetime even if he never saw her again.

"I have to go back home and take steps to prove to you and to myself that I can be a man who might someday be worthy of you, love," he said. It was a leap of faith, it was pretty much the scariest moment of his life.

Almost the scariest, he thought. Gazing down at the soft curves of her pale skin, the shining crown of her brown hair, breathing her into his pores so that she would remain there with him, he remembered those moments tonight when he had feared the worst. Somewhere a man with a gun had run off into the night after playing with everyone's lives. Somewhere another man had stolen a woman away in front of the eyes of a horrified audience. He would think about those things in time, and like everyone, he would worry. He would remember that moment of anguish when he'd thought the stolen woman had been Laura, when he hadn't known if she'd been in the line of fire, the moment his soul had screamed "Please, no." He would live those brief moments over and over, but for now, for this moment he would set that aside. For her. And whatever he answered, however much pain it cost him, he would abide by her decision. He'd never force her to see him if she didn't want it that way.

Laura's lovely green eyes widened. She leaned closer into his touch. "Prove yourself to me? Why? How do you intend to do that?"

He took a step back. It was too much, touching her this way. He didn't trust himself not to try and touch her more, bring her closer, sway her by skating his fingertips over sensitive nerve endings. That wouldn't be right.

"Dell has offered me a partnership in his construction firm," he managed to say. "I'm going to take it, Laura. I'm going to work hard to make sure you know that I can be a steady man, a man who'll always be there for the people he cares for."

And she smiled as if he'd said something funny. A shaky smile, but a smile. "You've always been there for the people you care for," she whispered. "You came here not just to help the Maitlands by keeping an eye on Clyde, but to save Clyde from himself if that became necessary. You kept your distance, so that Clyde would have a chance to save himself and have some pride. You're such a good son, Mick. And some-day you'll make some woman a wonderful husband when you find a lucky woman who deserves you.''

Oh, if only she hadn't said that, because there was no holding back now. He had to touch her, to hold her. Easing forward, Mick pulled Laura into his arms.

"It's never going to happen," he said solemnly. "I've already found the only woman I could love, and she doesn't want marriage."

"A woman who wouldn't want marriage to you? I don't believe it. Couldn't believe it," she said, her words coming out muffled where he cuddled her against his chest.

He shook his head, still holding on. "People have hurt the woman I love. She has good reasons for being wary and wanting to feel safe. I've got good reasons for keeping my distance. I don't ever want to be the man to hurt her. I want her safe, too."

Laura pulled back then and gazed up at him. A trace of tears misted her eyes. "Safe is definitely over-rated," she said. "I always wanted to be safe, and for weeks now I've felt that way because of you, but right now feeling safe isn't what's on my mind."

She tipped her chin higher, brought her body and her lips closer.

It was too much. He wanted her too badly. Mick brought his lips close, just hovering over her own. "You're a temptation, Laura," he whispered, his breath warming her. "It's going to be hell leaving you, but I have to prove myself to you."

She shook her head and their lips brushed slightly. "You don't have to prove a thing. I know everything I need to know."

Mick plowed his fingers into her hair. He looked deep into her eyes. "I hope you understand what you're saying, angel, because if I ask for you, I'm going to want forever. I'll want to marry you. I'll want to be a father to Meggie, and—"

She waited, the message in her eyes breaking his heart and filling him with hope.

"You're my world, love, the center of my being," he confessed. "I want to do the right thing. My head tells me that leaving you now *is* the right thing, but I want—" His voice grew thick. He faltered, tried to clear his throat and change his direction, say the right words.

She slid her arms up around his neck and shook her head. "Don't leave," she urged. "Please don't leave, Mick. Stay here and love me. Love *us*."

It was the closest he'd come to tears since Maeve's passing. It was the closest he'd ever come to heaven in his life.

Crushing her closer, he brought his lips down upon hers, hard at first, then gentling. Over and over, he brushed his lips against hers, angling his head, taking her mouth with his own. She was wine, she was a field of heady flowers, she was his. His lips claimed her, his body sang against hers, his mind spun, and his heart climbed a mountain and rejoiced.

Finally, he pulled back, smiling gently into her eyes.

"I think I've loved you from the very first," he said. "From that moment I caught you in my arms. Would you—that is, how would you feel if I decided to start a division of Dell Douglas Construction right here in Austin? Would that suit you?"

She laughed and he'd never heard a lovelier sound. "Having you beside me day and night would suit me," she confessed.

He smiled back, but only for a second. There was more to say. "I kept secrets from you," he reminded her.

Her smile didn't falter as she shook her head. "You didn't really. It wasn't a secret that you were keeping secrets. I knew all along. Your eyes—such wonderful eyes—your eyes don't lie."

A low chuckle escaped Mick. "My eyes don't lie, do they? Well, I wonder what they're saying right now."

"I hope they're saying, 'Come kiss me, love.'"

"Umm, they are," he said as he brought his lips as close as a breath and kissed her. "They're also saying, 'Come marry me, love.' Will you do that? Will you marry me?"

She kissed him first, the lightest of kisses, the sweetest of kisses. "I'll definitely marry you," she promised. "How could I not? I love you beyond belief. Besides, we've already shared the birth of a baby. Now we can go backward and share a wedding."

"And a wedding night."

"And the chance to make another baby?" she asked.

He bent her back and nuzzled just beneath the delicate curve of her jaw. "Let's make a lot of babies," he said, kissing his way back to her lips. "And when they're old enough—" he pulled back so that she could see the truth in his eyes "—I'll tell them how their mother stole my heart in the delivery room."

The sweetest smile and a sniffle was his reward. And then Laura rose on her toes. She kissed him long and sweetly, and she stole his heart all over again.

* * * * *

Was Blossom kidnapped
for her protection or another's?
Find out next month in
Stella Bagwell's exciting conclusion

THE MISSING MAITLAND (SR #1546).

MAITLAND MATERNITY

You loved the Maitland family. Now meet the long-lost Maitlands...!

In August 2001, Marie Ferrarella introduces Rafe Maitland, a rugged rancher with a little girl he'd do anything to keep, including—*gulp!*—get married, in **THE INHERITANCE**, a specially packaged story!

Look for it near Silhouette and Harlequin's single titles!

**Then meet Rafe's siblings in
Silhouette Romance® in the coming months:**

Myrna Mackenzie continues the story of the Maitlands with prodigal daughter Laura Maitland in September 2001's **A VERY SPECIAL DELIVERY**.

October 2001 brings the conclusion to this spin-off of the popular Maitland family series, reuniting black sheep Luke Maitland with his family in Stella Bagwell's **THE MISSING MAITLAND**.

Available at your favorite retail outlet.

Silhouette®
Where love comes alive™

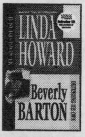

With help from
Silhouette's *New York Times*
bestselling authors
and receive a

FREE

Refresher Kit!
Retail Value of $25.00 U.S.

LUCIA IN LOVE by Heather Graham
and LION ON THE PROWL by Kasey Michaels

LOVE SONG FOR A RAVEN by Elizabeth Lowell
and THE FIVE-MINUTE BRIDE by Leanne Banks

MACKENZIE'S PLEASURE by Linda Howard
and DEFENDING HIS OWN by Beverly Barton

DARING MOVES by Linda Lael Miller
and MARRIAGE ON DEMAND by Susan Mallery

Don't miss out!

*Look for this exciting promotion, on sale in
October 2001 at your favorite retail outlet.
See inside books for details.*

Only from

Silhouette®

Where love comes alive™

Visit Silhouette at www.eHarlequin.com   PSNCP-POPR

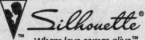

Feel like a star with Silhouette.

We will fly you and a guest to New York City for an exciting weekend stay at a glamorous 5-star hotel. Experience a refreshing day at one of New York's trendiest spas and have your photo taken by a professional. Plus, receive $1,000 U.S. spending money!

Flowers...long walks...dinner for two... how does Silhouette Books make romance come alive for you?

Send us a script, with 500 words or less, along with visuals (only drawings, magazine cutouts or photographs or combination thereof). Show us how Silhouette Makes Your Love Come Alive. Be creative and have fun. No purchase necessary. All entries must be clearly marked with your name, address and telephone number. All entries will become property of Silhouette and are not returnable. **Contest closes September 28, 2001.**

Please send your entry to: **Silhouette Makes You a Star!**

In U.S.A.
P.O. Box 9069
Buffalo, NY, 14269-9069

In Canada
P.O. Box 637
Fort Erie, ON, L2A 5X3

Look for contest details on the next page, by visiting www.eHarlequin.com or request a copy by sending a self-addressed envelope to the applicable address above. Contest open to Canadian and U.S. residents who are 18 or over. Void where prohibited.

Silhouette®
Where love comes alive™

Our lucky winner's photo will appear in a Silhouette ad. Join the fun!

SRMYAS1

HARLEQUIN "SILHOUETTE MAKES YOU A STAR!" CONTEST 1308
OFFICIAL RULES
NO PURCHASE NECESSARY TO ENTER

1. To enter, follow directions published in the offer to which you are responding. Contest begins June 1, 2001, and ends on September 28, 2001. Entries must be postmarked by September 28, 2001, and received by October 5, 2001. Enter by hand-printing (or typing) on an 8 ½" x 11" piece of paper your name, address (including zip code), contest number/name and attaching a script containing 500 words or less, along with drawings, photographs or magazine cutouts, or combinations thereof (i.e., collage) on no larger than 9" x 12" piece of paper, describing how the Silhouette books make romance come alive for you. Mail via first-class mail to: Harlequin "Silhouette Makes You a Star!" Contest 1308, (in the U.S.) P.O. Box 9069, Buffalo, NY 14269-9069, (in Canada) P.O. Box 637, Fort Erie, Ontario, Canada L2A 5X3. Limit one entry per person, household or organization.

2. Contests will be judged by a panel of members of the Harlequin editorial, marketing and public relations staff. Fifty percent of criteria will be judged against script and fifty percent will be judged against drawing, photographs and/or magazine cutouts. Judging criteria will be based on the following:

   - Sincerity—25%
   - Originality and Creativity—50%
   - Emotionally Compelling—25%

   In the event of a tie, duplicate prizes will be awarded. Decisions of the judges are final.

3. All entries become the property of Torstar Corp. and may be used for future promotional purposes. Entries will not be returned. No responsibility is assumed for lost, late, illegible, incomplete, inaccurate, nondelivered or misdirected mail.

4. Contest open only to residents of the U.S. (except Puerto Rico) and Canada who are 18 years of age or older, and is void wherever prohibited by law; all applicable laws and regulations apply. Any litigation within the Province of Quebec respecting the conduct or organization of a publicity contest may be submitted to the Régie des alcools, des courses et des jeux for a ruling. Any litigation respecting the awarding of a prize may be submitted to the Régie des alcools, des courses et des jeux only for the purpose of helping the parties reach a settlement. Employees and immediate family members of Torstar Corp. and D. L. Blair, Inc., their affiliates, subsidiaries and all other agencies, entities and persons connected with the use, marketing or conduct of this contest are not eligible to enter. Taxes on prizes are the sole responsibility of the winner. Acceptance of any prize offered constitutes permission to use winner's name, photograph or other likeness for the purposes of advertising, trade and promotion on behalf of Torstar Corp., its affiliates and subsidiaries without further compensation to the winner, unless prohibited by law.

5. Winner will be determined no later than November 30, 2001, and will be notified by mail. Winner will be required to sign and return an Affidavit of Eligibility/Release of Liability/Publicity Release form within 15 days after winner notification. Noncompliance within that time period may result in disqualification and an alternative winner may be selected. All travelers must execute a Release of Liability prior to ticketing and must possess required travel documents (e.g., passport, photo ID) where applicable. Trip must be booked by December 31, 2001, and completed within one year of notification. No substitution of prize permitted by winner. Torstar Corp. and D. L. Blair, Inc., their parents, affiliates and subsidiaries are not responsible for errors in printing of contest, entries and/or game pieces. In the event of printing or other errors that may result in unintended prize values or duplication of prizes, all affected game pieces or entries shall be null and void. **Purchase or acceptance of a product offer does not improve your chances of winning.**

6. Prizes: (1) Grand Prize—A 2-night/3-day trip for two (2) to New York City, including round-trip coach air transportation nearest winner's home and hotel accommodations (double occupancy) at The Plaza Hotel, a glamorous afternoon makeover at a trendy New York spa, $1,000 in U.S. spending money and an opportunity to have a professional photo taken and appear in a Silhouette advertisement (approximate retail value: $7,000). (10) Ten Runner-Up Prizes of gift packages (retail value $50 ea.). Prizes consist of only those items listed as part of the prize. Limit one prize per person. Prize is valued in U.S. currency.

7. For the name of the winner (available after December 31, 2001) send a self-addressed, stamped envelope to: Harlequin "Silhouette Makes You a Star!" Contest 1197 Winners, P.O. Box 4200 Blair, NE 68009-4200 or you may access the www.eHarlequin.com Web site through February 28, 2002.

Contest sponsored by Torstar Corp., P.O Box 9042, Buffalo, NY 14269-9042.

SRMYAS2

SILHOUETTE *Romance*

COMING NEXT MONTH

#1546 THE MISSING MAITLAND—Stella Bagwell
Maitland Maternity: The Prodigal Children
A mysterious man rescued TV reporter Blossom Woodward—and then kidnapped her! Blossom's nose for news knew there was more to Larkin the handyman than what he claimed…was he the missing Maitland they'd been searching for? Only *close* questioning could uncover the truth…!

#1547 WHEN THE LIGHTS WENT OUT…—Judy Christenberry
Having the Boss's Baby
Scared of small spaces, Sharon Davies turned to a stranger when she was stranded in an elevator, and got to know him *intimately*. Months later, she nearly fainted when she met her boss's biggest client. How could she tell Jack their time in the dark had created a little bundle of joy?

#1548 WORKING OVERTIME—Raye Morgan
Temporarily sharing a house with a woman and her toddlers awoke painful memories in Michael Greco, and sharing an office created more tension! The brooding tycoon tried to avoid Chareen Wolf and her sons, but eluding the boys was one thing—resisting their alluring mother was more difficult….

#1549 A GIRL, A GUY AND A LULLABY—Debrah Morris
A friend was all aspiring singer Ryanne Rieger was looking for when she returned to her hometown broke, disillusioned and pregnant. She found one in rancher Tom Hunnicutt. But Tom wouldn't be content with *just* friends—and could Ryanne ever let herself give more…?

#1550 TEN WAYS TO WIN HER MAN—Beverly Bird
Sparks flew the moment Danielle Harrington and Maxwell Padgett met. Strong willed and used to getting her own way, Danielle tried everything she could to make successful and sophisticated Max fall for her, except the one thing guaranteed to win his heart: being herself!

#1551 BORN TO BE A DAD—Martha Shields
Good Samaritan Rick McNeal became a temporary dad because of an accident. When Kate Burnett and little Joey needed a home, the lonely widower opened his door—but would he ever open his heart?

RSCNM0901